"You cannot marry him," he said, those dark green eyes so fierce, his face so hard.

It took Elena longer than it should have to clear her head, to hear him. To hear an insult no engaged woman should tolerate. It was that part that penetrated, finally. That made her fully comprehend the depths of her betrayal.

"Who are you?" she demanded. But she still let him hold her in his arms, as if she was something precious to him. Or wished she was. "What makes you think you can say something like that to me?"

"I am Alessandro Corretti," he bit out.

She stiffened, and his voice dropped to an urgent, insistent growl.

"And you know why I can say that. You feel this, too."

"Corretti…" she breathed, and the reality of what she was doing, the scope of her treachery, was like concrete blocks falling through her, one after the next.

He saw it, reading her too easily. His dark eyes flashed.

"You cannot marry him," he said again, with some kind of desperation beneath the autocratic demand in his voice. As if he knew her. As if he had the right. "He'll ruin you."

SICILY'S CORRETTI DYNASTY

The more powerful the family...the darker the secrets!

Mills & Boon® Modern™ Romance introduces the Correttis:

Sicily's most scandalous family!

Behind the closed doors of their opulent *palazzo*, ruthless desire and the lethal Corretti charm are alive and well.

We invite you to step over the threshold and enter the Correttis' dark and dazzling world...

The Empire
They're young, rich, and notoriously handsome—the Correttis' legendary exploits regularly feature in Sicily's tabloid pages!

The Scandal
But how long can their reputations withstand the glaring heat of the spotlight before the family's secrets are exposed?

The Legacy
Once nearly destroyed by the secrets cloaking their thirst for power, the new generation of Correttis are riding high again— and no disgrace or scandal will stand in their way...

Sicily's Corretti Dynasty

A LEGACY OF SECRETS
Carol Marinelli

AN INVITATION TO SIN
Sarah Morgan

A SHADOW OF GUILT
Abby Green

AN INHERITANCE OF SHAME
Kate Hewitt

A WHISPER OF DISGRACE
Sharon Kendrick

A FAÇADE TO SHATTER
Lynn Raye Harris

A SCANDAL IN THE HEADLINES
Caitlin Crews

A HUNGER FOR THE FORBIDDEN
Maisey Yates

8 volumes to collect—you won't want to miss out!

A SCANDAL IN THE HEADLINES

BY
CAITLIN CREWS

First published in Great Britain 2013
by Mills & Boon, an imprint of Harlequin (UK) Limited.
Harlequin (UK) Limited, Eton House, 18-24 Paradise Road,
Richmond, Surrey TW9 1SR

© Harlequin Books S.A. 2013

Special thanks and acknowledgement are given to Caitlin Crews for her contribution to *Sicily's Corretti Dynasty* series

ISBN: 978 0 263 23578 4

Caitlin Crews discovered her first romance novel at the age of twelve. It involved swashbuckling pirates, grand adventures, a heroine with rustling skirts and a mind of her own, and a seriously mouthwatering and masterful hero. The book (the title of which remains lost in the mists of time) made a serious impression. Caitlin was immediately smitten with romances and romance heroes—to the detriment of her middle school social life. And so began her life-long love affair with romance novels, many of which she insists on keeping near her at all times.

Caitlin has made her home in places as far-flung as York, England, and Atlanta, Georgia. She was raised near New York City, and fell in love with London on her first visit when she was a teenager. She has backpacked in Zimbabwe, been on safari in Botswana, and visited tiny villages in Namibia. She has, while visiting the place in question, declared her intention to live in Prague, Dublin, Paris, Athens, Nice, the Greek Islands, Rome, Venice, and/or any of the Hawaiian islands. Writing about exotic places seems like the next best thing to moving there.

She currently lives in California, with her animator/ comic book artist husband and their menagerie of ridiculous animals.

Recent titles by the same author:

A ROYAL WITHOUT RULES *(Royal & Ruthless)*
NO MORE SWEET SURRENDER
  (Scandal in the Spotlight)
A DEVIL IN DISGUISE
THE MAN BEHIND THE SCARS
  (The Santina Crown)

**Did you know these are also available as eBooks?
Visit www.millsandboon.co.uk**

CHAPTER ONE

"WHAT THE HELL are you doing on my boat?"

Elena Calderon froze in the act of polishing the luxurious teak bar in the yacht's upper lounge. The low growl of the male voice from across the room was laced with a stark and absolute authority that demanded instant obedience. And she knew exactly who he was without looking up. *She knew.*

She felt it slam into her, through her, like a sledgehammer.

Alessandro Corretti.

He wasn't supposed to be here, she thought wildly. He hadn't used this boat in over a year! He usually rented it out to wealthy foreigners instead!

"I'm polishing the bar," she managed to say. She kept her tone even because that was how a stewardess on a luxury yacht spoke to the guests. To say nothing of the owner himself. But she still couldn't bring herself to look at him.

He let out harsh kind of laugh. "Is this some kind of joke?"

"It's no joke." She tapped her fingers on the bar before her. "It's teak and holly, according to the chief steward."

She'd told herself repeatedly that what had happened during that one mad dance six months ago had been a fluke. More to do with the wine and the music and the romantic ballroom setting than the man—

But she didn't quite believe it. Warily, she looked up.

He was half-hidden in the shadows of the lounge's entryway, with all of that bright Sicilian sun blazing behind him—but she recognized him. A bolt of sensation sizzled over her skin, then beneath it, stealing her breath and setting off a hum deep and low inside.

Alessandro Corretti. The man who had blown her life to bits with one single dance. The man she knew was bad no matter how intensely attractive he was and no matter how drawn she was to him, against her will. The man who was even worse than her lying, violent, criminally inclined ex-fiancé, Niccolo.

Elena hadn't dared go to the *polizia* when she'd fled from Niccolo, fearing his family's connections. Alessandro's family, however, made those connections seem insubstantial, silly. They were the Correttis. They were above the law.

And yet when Alessandro stepped farther into the lounge, out of the shadows, Elena's chest tightened in immediate, helpless reaction—and none of it terror. Her breath caught. Her heart sped up. She yearned, just as she had six months ago, as if her body believed he was good. Safe.

"Was that an attempt at levity?" There was nothing in the least bit safe about his hard voice, or that look in his eyes. "Hilarious, I'm sure. But you still haven't answered my question, Elena."

Today the usually breathtakingly sophisticated eldest heir to and current CEO of Corretti Media and its vast empire looked…rumpled. Uncharacteristically disheveled, from his thick, messy dark hair to his scuffed shoes. His tall, muscled strength was contained in a morning suit with the torn jacket hanging open over his lean, hard chest. He had a black eye, scrapes and cuts that only accentuated his aristocratic cheekbones, a slightly puffy lip, even scraped knuckles. And that famous, cynical mouth of his was set in a grim line while his too-dark green eyes were ferociously narrowed. Directly at her.

What was truly hilarious, Elena thought then, was that she'd actually convinced herself he wouldn't recognize her in the unlikely event that they ran into each other on this yacht she'd been repeatedly assured he hardly used. She'd told herself that he had world-altering interactions like the one she wanted to forget with every woman he'd ever clapped eyes on. That it was simply what he did.

And if some intuitive, purely feminine part of her had whispered otherwise, she'd ignored it.

"I'm not trespassing," she said with a calm she wished she felt. "I work here."

"Like hell you do."

"And yet here I am." With a wave of her hand she indicated the smart tan-colored skirt she wore, the pristine black T-shirt tucked in at the waist, the sensible boat shoes. "Uniform and all."

His dark eyes were trained on her, hard and cold. She remembered the fire in them that night six months ago, the impossible longing, and felt the lack of both as a loss.

"You are…what, exactly? A maid?" His voice managed to be both incredulous and fierce at once, and she ordered herself not to react as he began to walk toward her, all impeccable male lines and sheer masculine poetry despite the beating he'd obviously taken.

Damn him. How could he still affect her like this? It disgusted her. She told herself what she felt now was *disgust*.

"I'm a stewardess. Cleaning is only one of my duties."

"Of course. And when you found yourself possessed

of the urge to trade in designer gowns and luxury cars for actual labor, I imagine it was pure coincidence that made you choose this particular yacht—my yacht—on which to begin your social experiment?"

"I didn't know it was yours." Not when she'd answered the original advert, when she'd decided waitressing at the tourist restaurants along the stunning Sicilian coast was too risky for someone who didn't want to be found. And now she wished she'd heeded her impulse to keep running when she'd discovered the truth. Why hadn't she? "When I found out, I'd already been working here a week. I was told you rarely, if ever, used it."

If she was honest, she'd also thought he owed her, somehow. She'd liked the idea that Alessandro had been paying her, however indirectly. That he was affected in some way by what that dance had put into motion, no matter if he never knew it. It had felt like a kind of power, and she needed every hint of that she could find.

"What a curious risk to take for so menial a position," he murmured.

He was even closer now, right there on the other side of the bar, and Elena swallowed hard when he put his hands down on the gleaming surface with the faintest hint of a sensual menace she didn't want to acknowledge. If she'd been on the same side he was, he would have been caging her between them. She couldn't seem to shake the image— or perhaps it was that the barrier seemed flimsy indeed when the way he was looking at her made something coil inside of her and pull taut.

"It's an honest job."

"Yes." His dark green gaze was laced through with something she might have called grief, were he anyone else. "But you are not an honest woman, are you?"

Elena couldn't hide the way she flinched at that, and she

wasn't sure what she hated more—that he saw it, or that she obviously cared what this man thought about her. When he didn't know anything about her. When all he'd ever known about her was that shocking, overwhelming explosion of awareness between them at that long-ago charity ball.

He couldn't know how bitterly she regretted her own complicity in what had happened that night, how her reaction to him still shamed her. He couldn't know what Niccolo had planned, what she'd very nearly helped him do. He knew how blind she'd been, sadly, but he couldn't know the truth....

But Alessandro was just like Niccolo, she reminded herself harshly then, no matter her physical reaction to him. Same kind of man, same kind of "family business," same kind of brutal exploitation of whoever and whatever he could use. She'd had a lot of time to read about Alessandro Corretti and the infamous Corretti family in her six months on the run. There was no telling what he might know about his rival Niccolo Falco's broken engagement and missing fiancée, or how he might use that information.

She had to be careful.

"I already know what you think of me," she said, keeping her voice cool. Unbothered. "And anyway, people change."

"Circumstances change." There was no denying the bitterness in his voice then, or stamped all over that battered, arrogant face. She told herself it didn't move her at all, that she didn't feel the insane, hastily checked urge to reach over and cover his hand with hers. "People never do."

Sadly, she knew he was right. Because if she'd changed at all—if she'd learned anything from these months of running and hiding—she wouldn't have found this man compelling in the least. She would have run screaming in the opposite direction, flung herself from the side of the boat and swum for the Palermo shoreline they'd left more than ninety minutes ago.

"If you don't want me here—"

"I don't."

She swallowed, fighting to remain calm. She couldn't afford to lose her temper, not when he could ruin everything with a single telephone call. It would take no more than that to summon Niccolo from that villa of his she'd nearly moved into outside of Naples. Alessandro would probably even enjoy throwing her back into that particular fire. Why not? The Correttis had been at bitter odds with Niccolo's family for generations. What was one more bit of collateral damage?

Especially when Alessandro already thought she was the sort of woman who aspired to be a pawn in the kind of games men like him played.

Think, she ordered herself. *Stop reacting to him and* think *about how best to play this!*

"Then I'll go, of course." Given what she knew he believed about her, he must imagine she'd be impervious to threats. Which meant she had to be exactly that. She smiled coolly. "But we're out at sea."

He shifted then, only slightly, and yet a new kind of danger seemed to shimmer in the air of the lounge, making Elena's pulse heat up and beat thick and wild beneath her skin. His dark green eyes gleamed.

"Then I certainly hope you can swim."

"I never learned," she lied. She tilted her head, let her smile flirt with him. "Are you offering me a lesson?"

"I suppose I can spare a lifeboat," he mused, that gleam in his eyes intensifying. "You'll wash up somewhere soon enough, I'm sure. The Mediterranean is a small sea." One corner of his battered mouth quirked up. "Relatively speaking."

She didn't understand how she could still find this man so beautiful, like one of the old gods sent down to earth again. Savage and seductive, even as he threatened to set her adrift. But she knew better than to believe her eyes, her traitorous body, that awful yearning that moved in her like white noise, louder by the second…. She knew what and who he was.

She shouldn't have had to keep reminding herself of that. But then, she couldn't understand why she wasn't afraid of him the way she'd come to be afraid of Niccolo, when she also knew Alessandro was far more dangerous than Niccolo could ever be.

"You're not going to toss me overboard," she said with quiet certainty.

A different kind of awareness tightened the air between them, reminding her again of that fateful dance. The way he'd held her so close, the things she'd simply *known* when she'd looked at him. That curve in his hard mouth deepened, as if he felt it, too. She knew he did, the way she'd known it then.

"Of course not," he said, those dark eyes much too hot, something far more alarming than temper in them now. Memories. That old longing. She had to be careful. "I have staff for that."

"Alternatively," she said, summoning up that smile again, forcing herself to stand there so calmly, so carelessly, "though less dramatically, I admit—you could simply let me go when we arrive at the next port."

He laughed then, and rubbed his hands over his bruised face. He winced slightly, as if he'd forgotten he was hurt.

"Maybe I'm not making myself clear." When he lowered his hands his gaze burned fierce and hot. She remembered that, too. And it swept through her in exactly the same way it had before, consuming her. Scalding her. "Niccolo

Falco's woman is not welcome here. Not on this boat, not on my island, not anywhere near me. So you swim or you float. Your choice."

"I understand," she said after a moment, making it sound as if he bored her. She should have been racked with panic. She should have been terrified. Instead, she shrugged. "You must have your little revenge. I rejected you, therefore you have to overreact and throw me off the side of a yacht." She rolled her eyes. "I understand that's how it works for men like you."

"Men like me," he repeated quietly, as if she'd cursed at him. He sounded tired when he spoke again, and it made something turn over inside of her. But she kept on.

"You're a Corretti," she said. "We both know what that means."

"Petty acts of revenge and the possibility of swimming lessons?" he asked dryly, but there were shadows in that dark gaze, shadows she couldn't let herself worry about, no matter that strange sensation inside of her.

"It also means you are well known to be as cruel and occasionally vicious as the rest of the crime syndicate you call your family." Her smile was brittle. "How lucky for me that I've encountered you on two such occasions."

"Ah, yes," he said, his dark gaze hard as his cynical mouth curved again, and something about that made her legs feel weak beneath her. "I remember this part. The personal attacks, the insulting comments about my family. You need a new topic of conversation, Elena."

He didn't move but, even so, she felt as if he loomed over her, around her, and she knew he was remembering it even as she did—those harsh words they'd thrown at each other in the middle of a ballroom in Rome, the wild flush she'd felt taking over her whole body, the way he'd only looked at her and sent that impossible, terrifying fire roaring through her. She felt it again now. Just as hot. Just as bright.

And just like then, it was much too tempting. She wanted to leap right into the heart of it, burn herself alive—

She shoved it aside, all of it, her heart pounding far too hard against her ribs. There was so much to lose if she didn't handle this situation correctly—if Niccolo found her. If she forgot what she was doing, and why. If she lost herself in Alessandro Corretti's dark, wild fire the way she still wanted to do, all these months later, despite what had happened since then.

"Far be it from me to stand in the way of your pettiness," she said, jerking her gaze from his and moving out from behind the bar. She headed for the doorway to the deck and the sunshine that beckoned, bright and clear. "It's a beautiful day for a swim, isn't it? Quite summery, really, for May. I'm sure I won't drown in such a small sea."

"Elena. Stop."

She ignored him and kept moving.

"Don't make me put my hands on you," he said then, almost conversationally, but the dark heat in it, the frank sensual promise, almost made her stumble. And, to her eternal shame, stop walking. "Who knows where that might lead? There are no chaperones here. No avid eyes to record our every move. No fiancé to watch jealously from the side of the dance floor. Which reminds me, are congratulations in order? Are you Signora Falco at last?"

Elena fought to breathe, to keep standing. To keep herself from telling this man—this dangerous, ruinous man— the truth the way every part of her screamed she should. She hardly knew him. She couldn't trust him. She didn't know what made her persist in thinking she could.

She thought of her parents—her loving mother and her poor, sick father—and what they must believe about her now, what Niccolo must have told them. The pain of that shot through her, taking her breath. And on some level, she knew, she deserved it. She thought about the unspoiled little village she'd come from, nestled on a rocky hill that ran along the sea, looking very much the same as it had hundreds of years ago. She needed to protect it. Because she was the only one who could. Because her foolishness, her selfishness and her vanity, had caused the problem in the first place.

She'd chosen this course when she'd run from Niccolo. She couldn't change it now. She didn't know what it was about Alessandro, even as surly and forbidding as he was today, that made her want to abandon everything, put herself in his hands, bask in that intense ruthlessness of his as if it could save her.

As if he could. Or would.

"No," she said. She cleared her throat. She had to be calm, cool. The woman he thought she was, unbothered by emotion, unaffected by sentiment. "Not yet."

"You've not yet had that *great honor*, then?"

She didn't know what demon possessed her then, but she looked back over her shoulder at him as if his words didn't sting. He was lounging back against the bar, gazing at her, and she knew what that fire in his eyes meant. She'd known in Rome, too. She felt the answering kick of heat deep in her core.

"I can't think of a greater one," she said. Lying through her teeth.

He watched her for a long, simmering moment, his gaze considering.

"And because you feel so honored you have decided to take a brief sabbatical from your engagement to tour the world as a stewardess on a yacht? My yacht, no less? When Europe is overrun by yachts this time of year, swarming like ants in every harbor, and only one of them belongs to me?"

"I always wished I'd taken a gap year before university," she said airily. Careless and offhanded. "This is my chance to remedy that."

"And tell me, Elena," he said, his voice curling all around her, tangling inside of her, making her despair of herself for all the ways he made her weak when she should have been completely immune to him, when she *wanted* to be immune to him, "what will happen when this little journey is complete? Will you race back into the *great honor* of your terrible marriage, grateful for the brief holiday? Docile and meek, as a pissant like Niccolo no doubt prefers?"

She didn't want to hear him talk about Niccolo. About the marriage he'd warned her against in such stark terms six months ago. It made something shudder deep inside of her, then begin to ache, and she didn't want to explore why that was. She never had.

This is not about you, she snapped at herself then, reminding herself how much more she had to lose this time. *And it's certainly not about him.*

"Of course," she said with an air of surprise, as if he really might believe that Niccolo Falco's fiancée was acting as a stewardess on a yacht simply to broaden her horizons before her marriage. As if she did. "I think that's the whole point."

"I've witnessed more than my share of terrible marriages," he said then, a bleakness beneath his voice and moving in his too-dark eyes as he regarded her. It made her shiver, though she tried to hide it. "I was only yesterday jilted at the start of one myself, as a matter of fact. My blushing bride was halfway down the aisle when she thought better of it." His mouth curved, cynical and hard.

"And yet yours, I guarantee you, will be worse. Much worse."

She didn't want to think about Alessandro's wedding, jilted groom or not. Much less her own. Once again, she fought back the strangest urge to explain, to tell him the truth about Niccolo, about her broken engagement. But he was not her friend. He was not a safe harbor. If anything, he was worse than Niccolo. Why was that so hard to keep in mind?

"I'm sorry about your wedding." It was the best she could do, and she was painfully aware that it wasn't even true.

"I'm not," he said, and she understood the tone he used then, at last, because she recognized it. *Self-loathing.* She blinked in surprise. "Not as sorry as I should be, and certainly not for the right reasons."

Alessandro straightened then, pushing away from the bar. He moved toward her—stalked toward her, if she was precise—and she turned all the way around to face him fully. As if that might dull the sheer force of him. Or her wild, helpless reaction to him that seemed to intensify the longer she was in his presence.

It did neither.

He stopped when he was much too close, that marvelous chest of his near enough that if she'd dared—if she'd taken leave of her senses entirely, if she'd lost what small grip she had left on what remained of her life—she could have tipped her head forward and pressed her mouth against that hard, beautiful expanse that she shouldn't have let herself notice in the first place.

"Tell me why you're here," he said in a deceptively quiet voice that made her knees feel like water. "And spare me the lies about gap-year adventures. I know exactly what kind of woman you are, Elena. Don't forget that. I never have."

There was no reason why that comment should have felt like he'd slapped her, when she already knew what he thought of her. When she was banking on it.

"You're hardly one to talk, are you? Remember that I know who you are, too."

"Wrong answer."

Elena sighed. "You were never meant to know I was here. Let me off when we reach port—any port—and it will be like I was never on this boat at all."

And for a moment, she almost believed he would do it.

That he would simply let it drop, this destructive awareness that hummed between them and the fact she'd turned up on his property. That he would shrug it off. But Alessandro's mouth curved again, slightly swollen and still so cynical, his eyes flashed cold, and she knew better.

"I don't think so," he said, his gaze moving from hers to trace her lips.

"Alessandro—" she began, but cut herself off when his gaze slammed back into hers. She jumped slightly, as if he'd touched her. She felt burned straight through to the core, as if he really had.

"I've never had someone try to spy on me so ineptly before," he told her in a whisper that still managed to convey all of that wild heat, all of that lush *want*, that she felt crackling between them and that would, she knew, be the end of her if she let it. The end of everything. "Congratulations, Elena. It's another first."

"Spy?" She made herself laugh. "Why would I spy on you?"

"Why would you want to marry an animal like Niccolo Falco?" He shrugged expansively, every inch an Italian male, but Elena wasn't fooled. She could see the steel in his gaze, that ruthlessness she knew was so much a part of him. Something else that reminded her of that dance. "You are a woman of mystery, made entirely of unknowables and impossibilities. But you can rest easy. I have no intention of letting you out of my sight."

He smiled then, not at all nicely, and Elena's heart plummeted straight down to her feet and crashed into the floor.

She was in serious trouble.

With Alessandro Corretti.

Again.

It was not until he propped himself up in the decadent outdoor shower off his vast master suite that Alessandro allowed himself to relax. To breathe.

The sprawling island house he'd built here on the small little spit of land, closer to the coast of Sicily than to Sardinia, was the only place he considered his true home. The only place the curse of being a Corretti couldn't touch him.

He shut his eyes and waited for the hot water to make him feel like himself again.

He wanted to forget. That joke of a wedding and Alessia Battaglia's betrayal of the deal they'd made to merge their high-profile families—and, of course, of him. To say nothing of his estranged cousin Matteo, her apparent lover. Then the drunken, angry night he hardly remembered, though the state of his face—and the snide commentary from the *polizia* this morning when he'd woken in a jail cell, hardly the image he liked to portray as the CEO of Corretti Media—told the tale eloquently.

His head still echoed with the nasty, insinuating questions from the paparazzi surrounding his building in Palermo when his brother, Santo, had taken him there this morning, merging with his leftover headache and all various agonies he was determined to ignore.

Did you know your fiancée was sleeping with your cousin? Your bitter rival?

Can the Corretti family weather yet another scandal?

How do the Corretti Media stockholders feel about your very public embarrassment—or your night in jail?

He wanted to forget. All of it. Because he didn't want to think about what a mess his deceitful would-be bride and scheming cousin had left behind. Or how he was ever going to clean it up.

And then there was Elena.

Those thoughtful blue eyes, the precise shade of a perfect Sicilian summer afternoon. The blond hair that he'd first seen swept up behind her to tumble down her back, that she'd worn today in a shorter tail at the nape of her neck. Her elegant body, slender and sleek, as enchanting in that absurd yachting uniform as when he'd first found himself poleaxed by the sight of her in that ballroom six months ago.

Then, she'd worn a stunning gown that had left her astonishingly naked from the nape of her neck to scant millimeters above the swell of her bottom. All of that silken skin *just there.*

His throat went dry at the memory, while the rest of his body hardened as it had the moment he'd laid eyes on her at that charity benefit in Rome. He didn't remember which charity it had been or why he'd attended it in the first place; he only remembered Elena.

"Careful," Santo had said with a laugh, seconds after Alessandro had caught sight of her standing only a few feet away in the crush of the European elite. "Don't you know who she is?"

"Mine," Alessandro had muttered, unable to pull his gaze away from her. Unable to get his bearings at all, as if the world had shuddered to a halt—and then she'd turned.

She'd looked around as if she'd been able to feel the heat of his gaze on her, and then her eyes had met his.

Alessandro had felt it like a hard punch in the gut. Hard, electric, almost incapacitating. He'd felt it—her—everywhere.

His.

She was supposed to be his.

He hadn't had the smallest doubt. And the fact that he'd acquiesced to his grandfather's wishes and agreed to a strategic, business-oriented marriage some two months before had not crossed his mind at all. Why should it have? The woman he was engaged to was as mindful of her duty and the benefits of their arrangement as he was. This, though—this was something else entirely.

And then he'd seen the man standing next to her, a possessive hand at her waist.

Niccolo Falco, of the arrogant Falco family that had given Alessandro's grandfather trouble in Naples many years before. Niccolo, who fancied himself some kind of player when he was really no more than the kind of petty criminal Alessandro most despised. Alessandro had hated him for years.

It was impossible that this woman—*his woman*—could have anything to do with scum like Niccolo.

"The rumor is her father has some untouched land on the Lazio coast north of Gaeta," Santo had said into his ear, seemingly unaware of the war Alessandro was fighting on the inside. "He is also quite ill. Niccolo thinks he's struck gold. Romance the daughter, marry her, then develop the land. As you do."

"Why am I not surprised that a pig like Niccolo would have to leverage a woman into marrying him?" Alessandro had snarled, jerking a drink from a passing waiter's tray and draining it in one gulp. He hadn't even tasted it. He'd seen only her. Wanted only her.

"Apparently that's going around," Santo had muttered.

Alessandro had only glared at him.

"Are you really going to marry that Battaglia girl in cold blood?" Santo had asked then, frowning, his dark green eyes so much like Alessandro's own. "Sacrifice yourself to one of the old man's plots?"

Santo was the only person alive who could speak to him like that. But Alessandro was a Corretti first, like it or not. Marrying a Battaglia was a part of that. It made sense for the family. It was his responsibility. He would marry for duty, not out of deceit.

Alessandro was not Niccolo Falco.

"I will do my duty," he had said. He'd tapped his empty glass to his brother's chest, smiling slightly when Santo took it from him. "A concept you should think about yourself, one of these days."

"Heaven forbid," Santo had replied, grinning.

The orchestra had started playing then, and Alessandro had ordered himself to walk away from the strange woman—*Niccolo Falco's woman*—no matter how bright her eyes were or how that simple fact made his chest ache. There was no possibility that he could start anything with a woman who was embroiled with the Falcos. It would ignite tempers, incite violence, call more attention to the dirty past Alessandro had been working so hard to put behind him.

Walking away had been the right thing to do. The only reasonable option.

But instead, he'd danced with her, and sealed his fate.

CHAPTER TWO

AND NOW SHE was here.

Alessandro had thought he was hallucinating when he'd first seen her on the yacht. He'd thought the stress was finally getting to him—that or the blows to his head. *You've finally snapped,* he'd told himself.

But his body had known better. It knew *her.*

He could still feel the heat of her when he'd touched her all those months ago, when he'd pulled her close to dance with her, when his fingers had skimmed that tempting hollow in the small of her back and made her breath come too fast. He still remembered her sweet, light scent, and how it had made him hunger to taste her, everywhere.

He still did. Even though there was no possible way that he could have ignored his responsibilities back then and pursued her, even if she hadn't been neck-deep in a rival family, engaged to one of the enemies of the Corretti empire. He'd told himself that all he'd wanted after that charity ball was to forget her, and he'd tried. God help him, but he'd tried. And there'd certainly been more than enough to occupy him.

There'd been the pressure of managing his grandfather's schemes, the high-profile wedding and the docklands regeneration project the old man had been so determined would unite the warring factions of the Corretti family.

"You will put an end to this damned feud," Salvatore had told him. "Brother against brother, cousins at war with one another. It's gone too far. It's no good."

It was still so hard to believe that he'd died only a few weeks ago, when Alessandro had always believed that crafty old Salvatore Corretti would live forever, somehow. But then again, it was just as well he'd missed that circus of a wedding yesterday.

And if Alessandro had woken from a dream or two over the past few months, haunted by clever eyes as blue as the sky, he'd ignored it. What he'd felt on that dance floor was impossible, insane.

The truth was, he'd never wanted that kind of mess in his life.

His late father, Carlo, had always claimed it was his intensity of emotion that made him do the terrible things he'd done—the other women, the shady dealings and violently corrupt solutions. Just as his mother, Carmela, had excused her own heinous acts—like the affair she'd confessed to yesterday that made Alessandro's adored sister, Rosa, his uncle's daughter—by blaming it on the hurt feelings Carlo's extramarital adventures had caused her.

Alessandro wanted no part of it.

He'd viewed his calm, dutiful marriage as a kind of relief. An escape from generations of misery. He was furious enough that Alessia Battaglia had left him at the altar—what would he have done if he had *felt* for her?

He'd felt far too much on a dance floor for a woman he couldn't respect. Far more than he'd believed he could. Far more than he should have. It still shook him.

Alessandro turned the water off and reached for a towel, letting the bright sun play over his body as he walked into his rooms. He didn't want to think about the wedding-that-wasn't. He didn't want to think about the things Santo had told him this morning en route to the marina—all the business implications of losing that connection with Alessia's father, the slimy politician who held the Corretti family's future in his greedy hands. He didn't want to think at all. He didn't want to feel those things that hovered there, right below the surface—his profound sense of personal failure chief among them.

And luckily, he didn't have to. Because Elena Calderon had delivered herself directly into his hands, the perfect distraction from all of his troubles.

He didn't care that she was almost certainly on some kind of pathetic mission from Niccolo and the Falco family, who had been openly jealous of the Corretti empire for decades. He didn't care why she was here. Only that she was when he'd thought her lost to him forever.

And he still wanted her, with that same wild ferocity that had haunted him all this time.

He'd had every intention of doing his duty to his family, to his grandfather's final wishes, and it had exploded in his face. Maybe it was time to think about what *he* wanted instead.

Maybe it was time to stop worrying about the consequences.

He found her in one of the many shaded, open areas that flowed seamlessly from inside to outside, making the whole house seem a part of the sea and the sky above. She was frowning out at the stretch of deep blue water as if she could call back the yacht he'd sent on its way with the force of her thoughts alone. He'd pulled on a pair of linen trousers and a soft white T-shirt, and he ran his fingers through his damp hair as she turned to him.

That same kick, hard to the gut and low. That same wildfire, that same storm.

His.

She looked almost vulnerable for a moment. Something about the softness of her full mouth, the shadows in her beautiful eyes. The urge to protect her roared through him, warring with the equally strong impulse to tear her open, learn her secrets—to figure out how she could want that jackass Niccolo, to start, and fail to see what kind of scum he was. How she could have felt what Alessandro had felt on that dance floor and turned her back on it the way she had.

How she did this to him when no other woman had ever got beneath his skin at all.

And there were no prying eyes here on his island. No whispers, no gossip. No one had to know she'd ever been here. There would be no business ramifications if he finally put his mouth on her. No ancient feuds to navigate, no humiliating scenes in public with his shareholders and the world looking on. Whatever game she and Niccolo were playing, it wouldn't affect Alessandro at all if he didn't let it.

No consequences. No problems. No reason at all not to do exactly as he wished.

At last.

"I told you to change into something more comfortable," he said, jerking his chin at that dowdy little uniform she still wore, not that it concealed her beauty in the least. Not that anything could. "Why didn't you?"

Clear blue eyes met his, and God, he wanted her. That same old fist of desire closed hard around him, then squeezed tight.

"I don't want to change."

"Is that an invitation?" he asked silkily, enjoying the way her cheeks flushed with the same heat he could feel climb in him. "Don't be coy, Elena. If you want me to take off your clothes, you need only ask."

* * *

His mocking words scalded her, then shamed her.

Because some terrible part of her wanted him to do it—wanted him to strip her right here in the sea air and who cared what came afterward? Some part of her had always wanted that, she acknowledged then. From the first moment their eyes had met.

Elena remembered what it had been like to touch this man, to feel his breath against her cheek, to feel the agonizingly sweet sweep of his hand over the bared skin of her back. She remembered the heat of him, the dizzying expanse of those shoulders in his gorgeous clothes, the impossible beauty of that hard mouth so close to hers.

It lived in her like an open flame. Like need.

She remembered what it had been like between them. For those few stolen moments, the music swelling all around them, making it seem preordained somehow. Huge and undeniable. Fated.

But look where it had led, that careless dance she knew even then she should have refused. Look what had come of it.

"No?" Alessandro looked amused. That sensual gleam in his dark green gaze tugged at her. Hard. "Are you sure?" His amusement deepened into something sardonic, and it didn't help that he looked sleek and dark and dangerous now, the pale colors he wore accentuating his rich olive skin and the taut, ridged wonder of his torso. "You look—"

"Thank you," she said, cutting him off almost primly. "I'm sure."

He really did smile then.

Alessandro sauntered toward her with all the arrogant confidence and ease that made him who he was, and that smile of his made it worse. It made him lethal. His shower had turned the evidence of his misspent night, all those cuts and bruises, into something very nearly rakish. Almost charming.

No one man should be this tempting. No other man ever was.

She had to pull herself together. The reality that she was trapped here, with Alessandro of all people, on this tiny island in the middle of the sea, had chipped a layer or two off the tough veneer she'd developed over the past few months. She was having trouble regaining her balance, remembering the role she knew she had to play to make it through this.

You will lose everything that matters to you if you don't snap out of this, she reminded herself harshly. *Everything that matters to the people you love. Is that what you want?*

He stopped when he stood next to her at the finely wrought rail that separated them from the cliff and the sea below. He was much too close. He smelled crisp and clean, and powerfully male. Elena could feel the connection between them, magnetic and insistent, surrounding them in its taut, mesmerizing pull.

And she had no doubt that Alessandro would use it against her if he could, this raging attraction. That was the kind of thing men like him did without blinking, and she needed to do the same. It didn't matter who she really was, how insane and unlike her this reaction to him had been from the start. It didn't matter what he would think of her—what he already did think of her. What so many others thought of her, too, in fact, or what she thought of herself. And while all of that was like a deep, black hole inside of her, yawning wider even now, she had to find a way to do this, anyway. All that mattered was saving her village, preserving forever what she'd put at risk in the first place.

What was her self-respect next to that? She'd given up her right to it when she'd been silly and flattered and vain enough to believe Niccolo's lies. There were consequences to bad choices, and this was hers.

"I should tell you," he said casually, as if he was commenting on the weather. The temperature. "I have no intention of letting you go this time. Not without a taste."

That was not anticipation that flooded through her then. And certainly not a knife-edge excitement that made her pulse flutter wildly in response. She wouldn't allow it.

"Is that an order?" she asked, her voice cool, as if he didn't get to her at all.

"If you like." He laughed. So arrogant, she thought. So sure of her. Of this. "If that's what gets you off."

"Because most people consider a boss ordering his employee to 'give him a taste' a bit unprofessional." She smiled pure ice at him. She did not think about what *got her off.* "There are other terms for it, of course. Legal ones."

He angled himself so he was leaning one hip against the rail, looking down at her. A faintly mocking curve to his mouth. Bruised and bad, head to foot. And yet still so terribly compelling. Why couldn't what she *knew* rid her of what she *felt*?

"Are we still maintaining that little bit of fiction?" He shrugged carelessly, though his gaze was hot. "Then consider yourself fired. Someone will find another stewardess for my yacht. You, however." His smile then made her blood heat, her traitorous body flush. "You, I think, have a different purpose here altogether."

Elena had to fight herself to focus, to remember. Alessandro Corretti was one of the notorious Sicilian Correttis. More than that, he was the oldest son of his generation, the heir to the legend, no matter how they'd split up the family fortune or the interfamily wars the press reported on so breathlessly. He was who Niccolo aspired to become—the real, genuine article. Corrupt and wicked to the marrow of his bones, by virtue of his blood alone.

He should have disgusted her to the core. He should have terrified her. It appalled her that he didn't. That nothing could break this hold he had on her. That she still felt this odd sense of safety when she was near him, despite all evidence to the contrary.

"Oh, right," she said now. "I forgot." She sighed, though her mind raced as she tried to think of what she would do if she really was the woman he thought she was. If she was that conniving, that amoral. "You think I'm a spy."

"I do."

No man, she thought unsteadily, should look that much like a wolf, or have dark green eyes that blazed when he looked at her that way. It turned her molten, all the way through.

"And what do you think spying on you would get me?"

"I know it will get you nothing. But I doubt you know that. And I'm sure your lover doesn't."

That he called Niccolo her lover made her skin crawl. That she'd had every intention of marrying Niccolo—and probably would have, had fate and this man and Niccolo's own temper not intervened—made her want to curl up into a ball and wail. Or tear off her own skin. But she tacked on a little smile instead, and pretended.

She got better at it all the time.

"You've caught me," she said. "You've unveiled my cunning master plan." She lifted her eyes heavenward. "I'm a spy. And I let myself be caught in the act of...stewardessing. Also part of my devious mission! What could I possibly want next?"

He looked amused again, which only made the ferocity he wore like a shield around him seem that much more pronounced.

"Access," he said easily. "Though I should warn you now, my computers require several layers of security, and if I catch you anywhere near them or near me when I'm having a private conversation, I'll lock you in a closet. Believe that, Elena, if nothing else."

He said that so casually, almost offhandedly, that smile playing around his gorgeous, battered mouth—but she believed him.

"You've clearly given my imaginary career in espionage a great deal of thought," she said carefully, as if she was appeasing a raving lunatic. "But ask yourself, why would I risk this? Or imagine you'd let me?"

His expression of amusement edged over into something else, something voracious and dark, and her pulse jumped beneath her skin.

"Your fiancé was not blind, all those months ago," he said softly. She felt him everywhere, again, as if he was touching her the way she knew he wanted to do. The way she couldn't help but wish he would. "Nor was I."

For a moment, she forgot herself. His dark green eyes were so fierce on hers then, searing into her. Challenging her. The world fell away and there was nothing but him and all the things she couldn't—wouldn't—tell him. All the things she shouldn't want.

And despite herself, she remembered.

Six months ago...

"Tell me your name," he demanded, sweeping her into his arms without even asking her if she'd like to dance with him.

Elena had seen the way he looked at her. She'd *felt* it, like a brand, a claim, from halfway across the room. She told herself that Niccolo, who had gone to fetch her a drink, wouldn't mind *one dance*. They were in full view of half of Rome. It was all perfectly innocent.

She knew she was lying. And yet, somehow, she didn't care.

He was stunning. Overwhelmingly masculine, impossibly attractive and, she thought with a kind of dazed amazement, *hers.* Somehow hers. He looked at her and set her alight. He touched her, and her whole body burst into a hectic storm of sensation, like being dropped headfirst into freezing cold water at the height of summer.

"Your name," he urged her. His hands were on her, hard and hot, making her shiver uncontrollably. His dark head was bent to hers, putting that mesmerizing mouth of his much too close. Tempting her almost past endurance.

"Elena," she whispered. "Elena Calderon."

He repeated it, and made it into something else. A kind of song. It swelled in her, changing her. It hung there between them, like a vow.

"I am Alessandro," he said, and then they'd danced.

He swept her along, every step perfect, his attention on Elena as if she was the only woman in the room. The only woman alive. Lightning struck everywhere they touched, and everywhere they did not, and some shameless, heedless part of her gloried in it, as if she'd been made for this. For only this. For him.

She felt him in the treacherous ache of her breasts, the unmistakable hunger low in her belly and the glazed heat that held her in its relentless grip as surely as he did. She *felt him*—and understood that what she was doing was wrong. Utterly, indisputably wrong.

She understood that she would have to live with this. That this was a defining moment. That her life would be divided into before and after this scorching hot dance, and that she would never again be the person she'd believed she was before this stranger pulled her against him. But his eyes were locked to hers, filled with wonder and fire, and she didn't pull away. She didn't even try—and she understood she'd have to live with that, too.

And then he made it all so much worse.

"You cannot marry him," he said, those dark green eyes so fierce, his face so hard.

It took her longer than it should have to clear her head, to hear him. To hear an insult no engaged woman should tolerate. It was that part that penetrated, finally. That made her fully comprehend the depths of her betrayal.

"Who are you?" she demanded. But she still let him hold her in his arms, like she was something precious to him. Or like she wished she was. "What makes you think you can say something like that to me?"

"I am Alessandro Corretti," he bit out. She stiffened, and his voice dropped to an urgent, insistent growl. "And you know why I can say that. You feel this, too."

"Corretti…" she breathed, the reality of what she was doing, the scope of her treachery, like concrete blocks falling through her one after the next.

He saw it, reading her too easily. His dark eyes flashed.

"You cannot marry him," he said again, some kind of desperation beneath the autocratic demand in his voice. As if he knew her. As if he had the right. "He'll ruin you."

Elena would never know what might have happened then, had she not jerked her gaze away from Alessandro's in confusion—and seen Niccolo there at the side of the dance floor, glaring at the two of them with murder in his black eyes.

Elena was amazed that it was possible to hate herself so much, so fully. And that the shame didn't kill her where she stood.

"How dare you?" she ground out, all her horror at her

own appalling actions in her voice. "I know who you are. I know *what* you are."

"What *I* am?" As if she'd stabbed him.

"Niccolo's told me all about you, and your family."

Something like a laugh. "Of course he has."

"The Correttis are nothing but a pack of violent thugs," she threw at him desperately, quoting Niccolo. "Criminals. One more stain on our country's honor."

"And Niccolo is the expert on honor, I suppose?" His face went thunderous, but his voice stayed cool. Quiet. Somehow, it made him that much more formidable. And it ripped into her like a knife.

"Do you think this will work?" she demanded, furious, and she convinced herself it was all directed at him. All *because* of him. "Do you really think you'll argue me into agreeing with you that *my fiancé*, the man I *love*, is some kind of—"

"You don't strike me as naive," he interrupted her, that fierce, dark edge in his voice, his gaze, even in his hands as he held her. "You must know better. You must."

He shook his head then, and she watched as bitter disappointment washed over him, turning his dark green eyes black. Making that fascinating mouth hard, nearly cruel. Making him look at her as if there had never been that fire between them, as if she couldn't still feel the flames, licking over her skin.

And she would never forgive herself, but she *ached.* She ached.

"Unless you like the money, the cars, the houses and the jewelry." His gaze was a jagged blade as it raked over her, and she bled. "The fancy dresses. Why ask where any of it comes from? Why face so many unpleasant truths?"

"Stop it!" she hissed at him.

"Ignorance is the best defense, I'm sure," he continued in that withering tone. "You can't be a stain on Italy's honor if you're careful not to know any of the sordid details, can you?"

None of this should be possible. A look, a dance, a few words with a total stranger—how could it *hurt?* How could she feel as if her whole world was ripping apart?

"You don't know what kind of woman I am," she told him, desperate to reclaim herself. To fix this. "And you never will. I have standards. I can't wait for Niccolo to do me the great honor of marrying me—to make me a Falco, too. I would never lower myself to Corretti scum like you. *Never.*"

He looked shattered for a moment, but only a moment. Then contempt moved over his fine, arrogant face, and made her stomach twist in an agony she shouldn't feel. He led her to the edge of the floor, gazed at her for one last, searing moment and then walked off into the crowd.

Elena told herself that wasn't grief she felt then, because it couldn't be. Not for a stranger. Not for a dance.

Not for a man she'd been so sure she'd never see again.

"I don't really remember," Elena said now in desperation, standing out on his terrace with only the sea to hear her lies. "It was a long time ago."

Alessandro only watched her, that wolf's smile sharp-edged, digging deep into her and leaving marks. He was much too close, and she hadn't forgotten a thing. Not a single thing.

"Then why are you blushing?" he asked, a knowing look on that battered, somehow even more attractive face—and her heart kicked hard against her ribs.

"I'm not spying on you," she gritted out, trying to break through the tension that gripped her. Trying to pretend he couldn't see into her so easily. "And if you really think I am, you should have let me leave with the boat."

But something had changed. His dark eyes burned. She felt the flames licking at her, seducing her and scaring her in equal measure.

"Alessandro." Saying his name was a mistake. She saw him react to it as if it was a caress, saw his intense focus on her sharpen, and it stole her breath away. "My being on your boat was a coincidence."

"Liar." Implacable. Fierce.

Elena's stomach knotted. She felt a deep kind of itch work through her, from her neck to her breasts to her core, and she felt a terrible panic bite at her then, as if she was in danger of losing herself completely.

You're supposed to be beating him at his own game! some last remnant of her self-control cried out inside her head.

"You can call me any names you like," she threw at him, desperate to find her balance again—to claw her way back to solid ground. "It won't change a thing. I met you once a long time ago. It wasn't particularly memorable."

That ruthless, cynical mouth kicked up in the corner, and his gaze turned jet black. It rolled through her, too hot to bear, shaking her apart from the inside out. Until there was nothing at all but this moment.

This. Him. Now.

"Such a liar," he whispered.

He reached out as if to touch her, but she knew she couldn't let that happen—*she couldn't*—so she threw out her own hand to catch his.

Skin against skin, after all this time. The same way their hands had touched once before, on that glimmering dance floor far away.

And they both caught fire.

The sea and the sun and the whole bright world disappeared into the blaze of it. There was only this man, who she should have run from the moment she'd seen him six months ago. This man, who had eyes like thunder and saw straight through into the heart of her. This man, who had claimed her from across a crowded room with a single, searing glance.

There was only the riot inside of her, the electricity that roared between them. *Skin to skin.* At last.

Neither one of them moved. Elena wasn't sure she breathed. This disastrous, unquenchable attraction seemed to swell and grow, radiating from his hand to hers, a hard, gnawing ache that every heartbeat only made worse. It penetrated every part of her, and made her want. Crave. *Need.*

"It haunts you," he said, a dark, male hunger stamped across his face. "I haunt you. Believe me, Elena. I know."

She jerked her hand from his. But as she did, she had a searing burst of clarity.

She wanted him. She always had. It didn't matter that it didn't make sense, that a single dance should never have affected her so much. It had. *He* had. And that wanting had ripped apart her world, changed everything. She'd been paying for it for six long months, in isolation and often in fear, moving from odd job to odd job across the whole of Italy, trying to keep herself out of sight and away from Niccolo.

All because of this. All because of Alessandro.

She had already been crucified for this crime. She paid for it every day. Why not commit it?

And if there was a part of her that knew that this was also the best way to prove to Alessandro that she was exactly the kind of woman he believed her to be, that this would cement his opinion of her, she told herself that only made the decision easier.

"This isn't a haunting," she whispered, watching the thunder roll through his eyes. "Neither one of us is a ghost." She smiled then. "I can prove it."

And then she indulged the roaring inside of her, that terrible hunger, and put her hands on him.

Not a light touch on his shoulder as she had when they'd danced, polite and appropriate. She slid her palms over the whisper-soft cotton that strained against his marvelous torso, and felt the pure, raw heat of him. The iron strength. Her head spun, dizzy and delicious.

Alessandro let out a sound that was almost a laugh, and then he tugged her closer, lifting her up against him. Her aching breasts pressed hard against his beautiful chest, sending a frantic shiver through her, and he muttered a curse. He settled her on the rail, his arms strong and hard and exquisite as they held her fast. She heard her boat shoes fall off, two loud slaps against the stone floor, and then she forgot them.

Alessandro stepped between her legs, and it wasn't enough. Her skirt kept him from pressing against her, into her, even as he leaned into the palms she'd flattened against him. She was surprised to see her hands were shaking. She was shaking. Or maybe the world was, all around them, and she didn't care.

This was finally happening. *Finally.*

He held her with one hand in the small of her back, hot and hard and *his*, while his other hand moved to her neck, her jaw, tracing patterns. Igniting her. And it wasn't *enough*—

"Look at me," he commanded her, that low voice of his snaking through her like a brushfire, making her skin seem to pull tight over her bones, and she would do anything. Anything he wanted. Anything at all.

Anything to keep them both burning like this.

His dark green eyes flashed, triumph and fire, and that wonder she knew was only theirs. Only this. His mouth looked nearly grim with need, and she knew she should be afraid. Of him. Of what was about to happen—what had always been going to happen, sooner or later.

But again, she felt only that wild passion. That desire. And that conviction that she was safer now, in his clever, dangerous hands, than she had been in months.

"Inevitable," she whispered before she knew she meant to speak, and the faintest hint of a smile moved across his mouth, then was gone.

"Hold on," he ordered her with a gruff intent that made her core seem to glow.

He moved his hands to cradle her face between them, and she grabbed his shirt in greedy fists.

At last, that voice chanted inside of her, again and again. *At last.*

And then he took her mouth with all of that ruthlessness and command, and Elena lost her mind.

CHAPTER THREE

HOT. WILD.

She was his.

And she kissed him back as if she wanted to devour him, too.

As if he'd set her on fire and this was how they'd burn, together, in this tumult of heat and glory, and her perfect mouth he couldn't taste enough.

She was better—this was better—than Alessandro had dared imagine in the middle of a hundred nights, when he'd pictured this in stark detail. When the dark fury that she could bewitch him as she had and be so much less of a person than he'd hoped didn't matter.

It didn't matter now, either. Need stormed through him, making him closer to desperate than he'd ever been before.

He wanted her skin against his, slick and sweet. He wanted his hands on those tempting breasts, her enchanting curves. He wanted to lick between her legs and stay there until she screamed. He wanted deep inside of her. *He wanted.* And every kiss, every taste, every little way she moved against him, only drove him higher.

"More," he said, and he picked her up again, yanking that damned skirt up and over her hips.

Deep masculine elation pounded through him when she lifted her legs and wrapped herself around him. And then he was there. Hard and hot against her melting heat, separated only by his trousers and the slightest wisp of material she wore. A delicate shudder moved through her, and for a moment he thought he might lose control.

But Alessandro wanted her too much, and had for too long. He took her mouth again, thrilled when she met him with a passion he could taste. She arched against him, her arms wrapped around his neck, and it wasn't enough.

It would never be enough.

He carried her to one of the loungers scattered about the terrace, then set her down. She was unsteady on her feet, her blue eyes wide and dazed, bright with need, and he wanted her more than he'd ever wanted anyone else. More than he'd imagined it was possible to want.

"Please," Elena said, her voice ragged with desire. The most beautiful thing he'd ever heard. "Don't stop."

Her hands were still on his chest, and he could feel each touch, each caress, directly in his sex. He kissed her again, deep and demanding, ravaging her mouth, and she thrilled him by returning it in kind.

Out of control. So good it hurt. Again. And again.

"These clothes need to come off," he muttered, pulling his mouth away from hers.

Alessandro moved to tug her T-shirt over her head, then hissed out a breath when he threw it aside and she stood there before him, bared to the waist. No bra to block him from her perfect breasts, small and round, with nipples like hard, ripe points. Lovely beyond reason. He nearly shook as his hands went to her skirt, working the zipper and then grabbing on to her panties as he tugged all of it down over her hips and out of his way.

And then Elena was naked. Gloriously, beautifully naked, and she was real and *here* and his. Finally his.

For a moment he only stared at her, a kind of awe sweeping through him as his body went wild, so desperate for her he could hardly bear it. He swept her up and then took her down with him, splaying her out above him as he lay back on the chaise.

Elena twisted against him, and then her frantic hands were on the hem of his T-shirt and he sat up slightly to peel it off. He brushed her hands out of the way to rid himself of his trousers, kicking them aside. And when he pulled her back into place they both sighed in something like reverence. And then she was like silk against him, all over him, soft and naked and hot.

Finally.

Alessandro's heart pounded. He was so hard it bordered on the painful, and then she rolled her hips and moved all of that slick, wet heat against the length of him, and he groaned. He traced the line of her spine down to her bottom, and then bent to take one of those achingly perfect nipples into his mouth. She made a wild, greedy sort of noise, and he couldn't wait. He couldn't take another moment of this magnificent torture.

It had been too long already. It had been forever.

He sat up, holding her against him, her soft thighs falling on either side of his. She knelt astride him, her hands moving from his chest to his shoulders, then burying themselves in his hair. Alessandro reached down between them, sinking his fingers deep inside the molten core of her.

She cried out, and he loved it. He tested her slickness, learned her lush shape, his palm hard against the center of her need. He watched her pretty face flush, felt her hips buck against his hand, and he returned to her breasts, sucking a taut nipple into his mouth and then biting down. Just hard enough.

She broke apart in his arms with a wordless cry, hot and wet in his hand, her head falling forward until her face was pressed into his neck. He lifted her in his arms while she still shook and shuddered, and then he thrust hard and deep inside her.

At last.

She was scalding hot, so deliciously soft, and still in the grips of her climax when he began to move. Alessandro held her hips in his hands and guided her into the rhythm he wanted. Slow, but demanding, catching the fire that was tearing her apart and building it up again with every stroke.

Higher. Hotter. Hungrier.

He heard her breath catch again, felt her stiffen, heard the shocked sound she made in his ear. She gripped his shoulders tight and shook all around him again, just as he wanted. He watched her arch back into the sunlight—so painfully, perfectly beautiful. This woman, *his woman*, lost to her pleasure, mindless and writhing against him, while he moved hard and deep inside of her.

He rolled them over on the lounger, coming on top of her and deeper into her. Alessandro let his head drop down next to hers, and then her arms wrapped around him, her hips meeting his in a wild, uncontrollable dance.

He felt her move beneath him, heard her gasp anew, and each hitch in her breath, each mindless cry, made him want her more. He was so deep inside of her, and they moved together like a dream—like a dream he'd had a thousand times, only much slicker, much hotter, much better.

And this time, when she began to break apart around him, when she threw her head back once more and arched up against him, Alessandro called out her name like the incantation it was and fell right along with her.

Elena came back to herself slowly. Painfully.

She was tucked up against Alessandro's side. He was sprawled out on the lounger beside her, one arm thrown over his head, looking for all the world like some kind of lazy, sated god. There was no reason he should be so appealing, even now, with his dark lashes closed, his arrogant features with the marks of the previous night's violence stamped into his skin. And yet...

She sat up gingerly, surprised her body still felt at all like her own when he'd made it his—made her his—with such devastating completeness. Her body still hummed with pleasure. So much pleasure Elena could hardly believe she'd survived it, that she was still in one piece.

Then again, perhaps she wasn't.

He shifted, and she felt his hand on her back, smoothing its way down to curl possessively over her hip. Impossibly, she felt something in her catch anew. A spark where there should have been nothing but ash and burned-out embers.

Surely this was the end of it. Succumbing to what had burned so bright between them had to have destroyed it, didn't it? But his fingers traced a lazy alphabet across her skin, spreading that fierce glow deep into her all over again, making her realize this wasn't over at all.

Elena had made a terrible mistake, she understood then. There were many ways to pay, and she'd just discovered a brand-new one. Perhaps, on some level, she'd held out the hope that what had surged between them was all smoke, no fire. That indulging it would defeat it.

Now she knew better. Now she knew exactly how hot they burned. She would have to live with that, too.

"Come here," he said, and she felt his voice move in her like magic, making her chest feel tight.

Despite herself, she turned. She looked down at him, bracing herself for a smug expression, a cocky smile—but that hard gaze of his was serious when it met hers. Almost contemplative. And that was worse, because she had no defense against it.

He reached up and traced a lazy line from her collarbone down over the upper swell of her breasts, and there was a dangerous gleam in his eyes when she caught his hand in hers and stopped him.

"Alessandro…" she began, but she didn't know what to say.

He didn't respond. Instead, he tugged her back down beside him, surrounding her once again with all that warm male strength. As if she were safe, she thought in a kind of despair. As if she'd finally come home.

When she knew perfectly well neither one of those things were true.

His gaze darkened as he watched her. He slid a hand around to the nape of her neck, but she was the one who closed the distance between them, pressing her mouth to his, spurred on by a great wealth of emotion she didn't want to understand.

This time, there should have been no wild explosion, no impossible heat. This time, she should have been more in control of herself, of all these things she didn't want to feel.

But his mouth moved on hers and something incandescent poured through her, lighting her up all over again. She felt that spark ignite, felt that same fire grow again inside of her. His kiss was tender, something like loving, and it ripped her into pieces.

She kissed him back, desperately, letting her hands learn his fascinating body all over again, letting herself disappear into this madness that she knew perfectly well would destroy her. It was only a matter of time.

And this time when he slid into her it was a different kind of fire. Slow, deliberate. It stripped her bare, made her eyes fill with tears, battered what was left of her defenses, her carefully constructed veneers. He gazed down at her as he moved inside of her, his dark eyes grave and something more she didn't want to name, as he spun this wicked fire around them.

As he wrecked her totally, inside and out, and she loved every second of it.

And then he pushed them both straight over the edge of the world.

When she woke a second time, the sun was beginning to sink toward the sea, bathing the sky in peaches and golds, and Alessandro wasn't next to her. Elena sat up in confusion, only realizing as she almost let it slide from her that she was draped in something deliciously silky. A robe, she discovered when she frowned down at it.

She pulled it on as she stood, belting it around her waist, and when she looked up she saw him.

He sat at a nearby table in the gathering dusk, a wineglass in one hand, his gaze trained on her. He hadn't bothered with his shirt. A quick glance assured her he was wearing those loose, soft trousers, low on his narrow hips. That lean, smoothly muscled body was even more beautiful from a distance and now, of course, she knew what he could do with it. *She knew.* She snapped her attention back to his face—and went still.

He was watching her with an expression that made her breath catch in her throat. She recognized that look. This was the Alessandro Corretti she remembered, brooding and dark.

And it seemed he'd remembered that he hated her.

Elena steeled herself. It was better this way. This was what she'd wanted. She ran her hands down the front of the silk robe, but then stopped, not wanting him to see any hint of her agitation.

"Sit down," he said, indicating the table before him and the selection of platters spread out across its inlaid mosaic surface. His voice was cold. Impersonal. A slap after what they'd shared, and she was sure he knew it. "You must be hungry."

The moment he said it she realized she was ravenous, and she told herself that was the only reason she obeyed him and sat. Alessandro seethed with a dark menace, lounging there with such studied carelessness, watching her with a slight curl to his lip.

She'd expected this, she reminded herself. She'd known sleeping with him would make him despise her, would confirm his low opinion of her, when he believed her still engaged to Niccolo and all manner of other, horrible things. But it shocked her how much it hurt to see it, how it clawed into her, threatening to spill out of her eyes. She blinked it away.

And then she settled herself in the seat across from him as if she hadn't a care in the world, and gazed down at the food spread out before her. A plate of plump, ripe cheeses, tangy cured meats and an assortment of thick, lush spreads—an olive tapenade, a fragrant Greek-style taramasalata—next to a basket of fresh, golden semolina bread. A serving dish piled high with what looked like an interesting take on the traditional Sicilian caponata, a cooked aubergine salad laden here with succulent morsels of seafood, rich black and green olives and sweet asparagus spears.

Elena took the wine he poured for her, a rich and hearty red, and sipped at it, letting the mellow taste wash over her, wash her clean. She tried to match his seeming insouciance, leaning back in her chair and holding her glass airily, as if she spent most of her evenings with her various lovers in their magnificent island estates. As if this—as if he—was nothing but run of the mill.

"It's quite good," she said, because she thought she should say something.

Not for the first time, she was painfully aware of how deeply unsophisticated she really was—how categorically unsuited to playing in these deep, dark waters with men like him. Niccolo had dressed her up and taught her how to play the part, but here, now, she was forcefully reminded that she was only Elena Calderon, a nobody from a remote village no one had ever heard of, descended from a long line of mostly fishermen. She was out of her league, and then some.

Alessandro only watched her. Something about that cold regard, that dark, silent fury, made her feel raw. Restless.

"Alessandro Corretti with nothing to say?" She attempted a smile. "Shocking."

"Tell me," he said in that calm, easy way that only emphasized the deadly edge beneath. "When you run back to your fiancé and tell him what you did here, how detailed a picture will you paint for him? When you tell him you slept with a man he loathes, will you also tell him how many times you screamed my name?"

Elena paled, even though she knew she shouldn't—that she should have expected this. That she *had* expected this. Her fingers clenched hard on the stem of her glass.

"Or perhaps that's how he likes it. Perhaps he enjoys picturing his woman naked and weeping with ecstasy in another man's arms." His eyes were like coals, hot and black. "Perhaps this is a game the two of you play, and I am only the latest in a long line of targets. Perhaps you are the bullet he aims at his enemies, then laughs about it later."

Elena congratulated herself on achieving precisely what she'd set out to achieve, and in spades. She told herself his opinion of her didn't matter. That the worse it was, the better. The less he thought of her, the less he'd feel compelled to betray her to Niccolo. She took another nonchalant sip of her wine, and ordered herself to enjoy her curiously bitter-tasting triumph.

"Niccolo is a man of many passions," she said, and was perversely satisfied by the flash of temper in his gaze.

"Never mind what that makes you."

She glared at him, determined not to let him see he'd landed a blow. She reminded herself that she could only be used as a bargaining chip if he believed she had some worth.

"Are you calling me a whore?" she asked softly. *This is good,* she assured herself. *This is what you want.*

But even the air seemed painful, shattering all around her. As if it was as broken as she felt.

"Is this some kind of twisted retribution for Rome?" he asked after long moments passed, no hint of green in those dark eyes of his.

"I'm not the one who started this," Elena threw at him before she had time to consider it. Not that he was the first man to think she was a whore, not that Niccolo hadn't covered the same ground extensively—but somehow, this didn't feel anything like the triumph it should have been. It hurt. "I was perfectly happy on that boat. But you had to sweep in and ruin everything, the same way you did—"

She cut herself off, appalled at what she'd nearly said. Her heart was rioting in her chest, and she was afraid to look at him—afraid of what she'd see. Or what he would.

"By all means," he invited her, his voice silk and stone. "Finish what you were saying. What else did I ruin?"

She would never know how she pulled herself together then, enough to look at him with clear eyes and something like a smile on her mouth.

"That was the first ball I'd ever attended, my first night

in Rome," she said, light and something like airy, daring him to refute her. "I felt like a princess. And you ruined it."

"You have no comprehension whatsoever of the damage you do, do you?" He shook his head. "You're like an earthquake, leaving nothing but rubble in your wake."

It's like he knows, a little voice whispered, directly into that dark place inside of her where she hated herself the most. *Like he knows what you nearly let happen.*

She set her glass back down on the table with a sharp click. "I don't know what you want from me."

"I would have thought that much was clear," he replied, a self-mocking curve to that hard mouth she knew too well now. Far too well. "If nothing else. I want you, Elena. Then. Now. Still. God help us both."

Elena clenched her hands together in her lap, everything inside of her seeming to squeeze tight and *ache.* Something deep and heavy sat over the table as the sun disappeared for good, and soft lights came on to illuminate the terrace. She could feel it pressing down on her, into her, and the way he was looking at her didn't help.

"No clever reply to that?" His voice then was quiet, yet no less lethal, and it sliced into her like a jagged blade. "I don't know what lies you tell yourself. I can't imagine. But I know you want me, too."

She shook her head as if that might clear it, pulling in a breath as if that might help. When she looked at him again, she wasn't playing her part. She couldn't.

"I want you," she said in a low voice, letting all of the ways she loathed herself show, letting it all bleed out between them, letting it poison him, too. "I always have. And I'll never forgive myself for it."

She thought he looked shaken then, for the briefest moment, but he blinked it away. And he was too hard again, too fierce. She told herself she'd seen only what she wanted to see. He sat forward, those dark, cruel eyes fixed on her, and she reminded herself that nothing shook this man. Nothing could. Especially not minor little earthquakes like her.

"Congratulations, Elena," he said, his voice a sardonic lash. "I believe that's the first honest thing you've said to me since you told me your name."

She had to wrench her gaze away from his then, while she ordered herself to stay calm. To tamp down the chaotic emotions that surged inside of her, taking her over, making her want nothing more than to sob—once again— for something she could never have. Something she never should have wanted in the first place.

Unbidden, images of what they'd done together, here on this very same terrace, skated through her mind. His mouth, those hands. The wild heat of him, his impossible strength and his ruthless, intense possession—

Something occurred to her then, slamming through her as hard and as vicious as if he'd punched her in the gut. He might as well have. It couldn't have been worse.

She had been on birth control pills throughout her relationship with Niccolo, but the past six months had been so hectic. She'd run away and run out of the pills, and she hadn't wanted to leave any kind of record of where she'd been—so no doctors. She hadn't imagined it would be an issue. And then, today, she'd simply forgotten she wasn't protected.

She'd forgotten.

"We didn't use anything," she gasped out, so appalled she could hardly get the words past her lips. She felt numb with horror.

Alessandro went still. Too still. And for the first time in their brief, impossible acquaintance, she couldn't read a thing in the narrow, considering gaze he aimed at her. She could only see the darkness.

"I'm clean," he said. Cool and concise. And nothing more.

And the caustic slap of that helped her, strangely. It reminded her who she was, what she was doing here. Why she'd decided to give in to her desire for him in the first place.

"You think I'm a liar and I know very well you are," she said, trying for a calm tone. "You'll excuse me if I have no particular reason to believe you."

Temper streaked across that arrogant face of his. "You know I'm a liar, do you?" His deceptively gentle tone made her skin prickle. "And how exactly do you know that?"

She laughed, deliberately callous. "Because I know your name."

A deep blackness flashed through his dark green eyes and over his face then, old and resigned, with the faint hint of some kind of pain, and Elena fought off a sharp stab of regret. She shouldn't care if she hurt this man's feelings. He certainly didn't care if he hurt hers. So why couldn't she stave off the bizarre urge to apologize? To trust him the way that insane part of her urged her to do?

But even as she opened her mouth to do exactly that, she stopped herself. Because their carelessness had changed everything. She knew enough about him to know that he would never send her back to Niccolo if he thought she might be carrying his baby. Not a proud man like Alessandro. Not when the blood between the Falcos and the Correttis had been notoriously bad for generations.

Which meant, after all of this, she really was as safe as she'd always felt with him.

It should have felt something more than hollow.

But she had to keep going no matter how it felt. She had

to push this to its logical extreme. This was her chance to stay hidden away in a place Niccolo could never find her. In a place he'd never dream or dare to look.

"I could be pregnant," she said, steeling herself to the look on his face then, to her own intense horror at what she was doing. But she had no other option. There was so little time left, and she couldn't let Niccolo find her. She would do anything to keep that from happening, even this.

"I'm familiar with the risks," Alessandro bit out, temper still dark on his face, in his eyes, shading his firm mouth. "Why the hell aren't you protected?"

Elena eyed him across the table. "I wasn't aware that the sole responsibility for protection fell to me. Were you not equally involved?"

He muttered a harsh, Sicilian word beneath his breath, and she was perfectly happy she couldn't understand the dialect even after her time there.

She reached out to one of the platters, scooping up some of the olive tapenade with a piece of the fragrant bread and settling back to nibble at it as if she hadn't a care in the world.

"It will be fine, I'm sure," she said. She met his gaze and allowed herself a callous smirk. "Niccolo will never know the difference."

Alessandro actually jerked in his chair. His face went white.

"Over my dead body will you pass off a child of mine as his," he said hoarsely, so furious he nearly lit up the night with it. "Over my dead body, Elena—or yours."

She smiled. It didn't matter that he looked at her as if she revolted him completely. It didn't matter that she hated herself, that she thought she might be sick from this terrible manipulation. It didn't even matter that she really might be pregnant, which she couldn't let herself consider. It only mattered that she kept herself safe, one way or another, for this little while longer. Whatever the cost.

And the truth was, she knew somehow Alessandro would never hurt her. Hate her, perhaps, but never hurt her, and after all these months that was the same thing as safe. And it was a far better bargain than being with a man like Niccolo, who had pretended to love her and would likely put her in the hospital if he caught up with her.

"Then we'll count a month from today," she said smoothly, as if she'd never had any doubt that it would end this way. That she would get what she wanted. "Plus an extra ten days or so, as these things are so inexact. And we'll see if any dead bodies are necessary, won't we?"

His jaw was tight and hard, his gaze like bullets. "Forty days. On my island. Alone. With me."

He stared at her for a long moment, and she made herself look back at him, shameless and terrible, the woman he'd always believed she was and far worse than he'd imagined. This was her protection. This brazen, horrible creature she'd become, this calculated act. This was how she'd save herself, and the things she held dear.

"Or I could text you," she offered.

His face was drawn, that serious mouth grim. And his eyes were like the night around them, haunted and destroyed. This was what she'd done. This was what security looked like.

This was one more thing she'd have to live with when all of this was done.

"Just remember," he said, threat and promise laced through that low voice, bright in his dark eyes. "You asked for this."

CHAPTER FOUR

IT WAS WORSE now that he knew, Alessandro thought days later.

Worse now that he'd touched her, tasted her, held her. Lost himself inside her. There was no unknowing her exquisite heat, her lithe body wrapped around his as if she'd been created for that alone. For him. There was no forgetting it.

Alessandro didn't understand how he could know what he knew and still want her. How she could have used their carelessness as leverage, making him wonder if it had been carelessness on her part at all—and yet, he still wanted her.

He sickened himself.

"You don't need to look at me like that," she'd said the other morning out by the pool, not looking up from the glossy English magazine he assumed one of his unfailingly efficient staff had provided for her. Better to focus on that than what she looked like in a scalding red bikini hardly big enough to lick over the curves it displayed. Better to ignore how much he wanted to lick those curves himself. "I'm aware of what you think of me. The dark and terrible glare is overkill."

"This glare is the only thing between you and my temper," he'd replied, making no attempt to cushion her from the thrust of that temper in his voice. "I'd be more grateful for it, were I you."

"And what will you do if you lose it?" Elena had asked, sounding bored. She'd angled a look at him then over the rims of her dark glasses. "Hate me even more? By all means. Try."

It had taken everything he had not to cross over to her then and there and teach her exactly where his temper would lead. Exactly where it would take them both. The hot glory of the way they could burn each other alive. Only the fact that he wanted it too badly, and was furious at himself for that shocking deficiency in his character, kept him from it.

Alessandro stood up on one of the terraces now, looking out over the sweep of land that made up the rest of the island behind his house. On the far side of the tennis court was the small meadow that ran down to the rocky shore, late-spring grasses and early-summer flowers preening beneath the June sun. Scrappy pines and elegant palm trees scraped the sky. Stout fruit trees displayed their wares— lemons and oranges and leafy almonds. Seagulls floated in the wind, calling out their lonely little songs. And in the center of all that natural beauty was Elena.

Elena. Always Elena.

He'd been so furious that first night he was glad she'd removed herself shortly after dropping her little bombshell about her possible pregnancy—and her intention to stay here, with him. He'd drunk his way into what passed for sleep and had woken the next morning determined to regain the upper hand he never should have yielded in the first place.

She wanted to stay on his island to further some twisted agenda of her own? She wanted to play this game of consequences with him? *Va bene.* Then she would have to deal with what she'd put into action. And she'd have to face him while she did it.

"I'll expect you at dinner," he'd told her that first morning. "Every night."

She'd been walking into the cheerful breakfast room then, its floor-to-ceiling glass windows pulled back to let the morning in. She'd hardly looked at him as she'd helped herself to the carafe of the strong Indonesian coffee he preferred to the more traditional, milky cappuccinos.

"Your expectations are your own, Alessandro," she'd said almost sweetly when she'd turned back from the simple, wood-carved sideboard to face him, balancing her coffee cup in her hands.

She'd worn a huge, shapeless sundress, swaddling herself in cheery turquoise from her neck to her toes, and topped off with one of those flimsy, gauzy wrap things that served no discernible purpose at all but to conceal her figure.

He'd liked the idea that she'd felt she had to hide herself from him. That he'd got at least that far beneath her treacherous skin, that he hadn't been the only one feeling battered that morning.

"If you want to hold me captive on my own island for forty days, that's the price."

"The price is too high."

He'd smiled. "You really won't like my alternate plan. Trust me."

"I told you I'd be happy to go my merry way and let you know what happens," she'd replied, her expression cool but her blue eyes a shade darker than usual. "You were the one who started ranting on about dead bodies. I don't see why I should have to subject myself to more of the same over dinner."

"Afraid you won't be able to control yourself?" he'd

taunted her. "Will I be forced to fend off your advances over pasta alla Norma, Elena? Defend what remains of my virtue over the soup?"

Her blue eyes had blazed. "Unlikely."

"Then I fail to see the problem," he'd said, still smiling, though his gaze had been a challenge and demand on hers.

Her mouth had curved slightly then, that cool slap of a smile he'd already come to loathe.

"Also unlikely," she'd replied.

He'd lounged there in his chair and looked at her for a moment, enjoying himself despite the pounding in his head, the stark disillusionment in his heart. Despite what he knew about her now. Despite his own weakness for her that even her distasteful manipulations couldn't erase.

"I warned you," he'd said softly. Deliberately. "You wanted this."

"I wanted—" But she'd thought better of whatever she'd been about to say, and had pressed her lips together.

"Be careful what you wish for next, *cara,*" he'd advised her silkily. "You might get that, too."

Alessandro moved farther out on the terrace now, frowning down at her. That exchange had been days ago. He'd spent a good hour this morning working out his weakness in his pool, swimming lap after lap and still not managing to shift this thing off him that made him want her like this. That made him hunger for her no matter how little he liked her.

That made him *long* and *yearn* and *wish*, like he was someone else entirely.

Or as if she was.

She sat out in his sweet-smelling meadow on a bright orange blanket, her eyes closed and her head tipped back, soaking in the sunshine like some kind of flower. Like something utterly innocent, clean and pure. His mouth twisted. She wore a short, flirty dress in a pale yellow color that left her golden-skinned arms and legs bare, then tucked in at her delectable waist to highlight the unmistakable elegance of her lean, slender form.

He let his gaze trace the beautiful lines of her face, that perfectly lush mouth and the loose waves of the blond hair that she hadn't pulled back again since that first night. It danced around her in the ocean breeze, the color of country butter with hints of white-blond, as well, and he hated that she could be so pretty, so effortlessly lovely, when he knew the sordid truth about her.

She was engaged to Niccolo Falco, and she'd slept with him, anyway.

He couldn't understand why that alone wasn't the end of this pitched battle inside of him. Why that simple fact didn't end this need for her that still burned him up and kept him from his sleep. It should have been all he needed to dismiss her from his thoughts entirely. He was not the kind of man who enjoyed poaching, unlike his cousin Matteo. He got no pleasure from finding himself in the middle of other people's relationships. Life was complicated enough, he'd always thought, and his own parents' squalid legacy had seemed to confirm it. Why cause himself more trouble?

After all, he had more than his share already. It was his birthright.

He'd spent the bulk of the morning fuming over his voice mail and most of his text and email messages, sending his beleaguered assistant increasingly terse instructions to deal with whatever came up as best he could, and not to bother Alessandro with any of it unless it was an emergency. An objectively dire one. The various pleas and attempts to draw him out from friends and family he deleted without a reply—all except for Santo, who got a terse line indicating that Alessandro was alive, and only because his messages had focused on Alessandro's well-being instead of the family.

His goddamned family.

He wasn't coming home to sort out the cursed business deal his aborted wedding had left in tatters. He didn't want to know that his illegitimate half-brother, Angelo, ignored all his life by their father and understandably furious about it, was making his move at last. He wasn't interested in what the latest Corretti family scandal was now that he'd removed himself. He didn't want to hear his mother's pathetic excuses for the way she'd savaged his sister, Rosa, in earshot of most of Palermo society, dropping the truth of her parentage on her like a loud, drunken guillotine. He didn't care where his runaway bride had gone and he certainly didn't want to join in the speculation about whether or not his cousin Matteo had gone with her.

He wanted to be numb. He wanted to encase himself in ice and steel and feel nothing, ever again. No useless sense of duty. No pathetic compulsion to play the rescuer, the hero, for his endlessly needy family members, none of whom ever quite appreciated it. No useless longing for a woman who neither deserved it nor wanted it.

No wondering what it was in him that was so twisted, so ruined and corrupt and despicable, that the bride he'd carefully arranged and contracted abandoned him at the altar and the beautiful stranger he'd fallen for so disastrously at a glance wanted nothing more than to use him for her own ends.

He wanted to be numb.

But if he couldn't be numb, he decided then, staring down at her luxuriating in all of that sunlight, he might as well explore that darkness inside of him that he'd fought his whole life.

Elena wanted to play her games with him. Dangerous games, because she thought she was dealing with another brutish thug like her fiancé. Maybe he should give her what she wanted. Maybe he should bring out the whole of his arsenal in return.

Maybe it was finally time to be who he was: a Corretti, callous and selfish, destined for nothing but depravity from the moment of his birth.

Just like all the rest of them. Just like the father he'd always despised.

"I want to be inside you," Alessandro said casually. He was standing at the windows, his back to her. "Now."

Elena froze in her seat. She set her fork down carefully.

She'd grown used to these long, fraught meals they shared each night, prodding each other for weaknesses. She'd come to enjoy the strange exhilaration she got from matching wits with him, so different from meals with Niccolo—who had done the talking while she'd sat there adoringly, grateful for her good luck.

She'd grown used to the dark looks he sent her way whenever he saw her, cold condemnation and a banked fury, a far cry from the flat coldness she'd once seen in Niccolo's eyes, moments before he'd showed her who he really was. She'd told herself she was used to this by now. To Alessandro himself. To all this forced exposure to the man who had chased her through dreams for six long months.

"I gave in to that urge once already," she murmured. "And look what's happened."

She hadn't thought to worry about sex.

She hadn't imagined it would be an issue, after that first day. He'd looked at her as if he'd rather die than touch her again, and she'd told herself she was glad of it.

Of course she was.

"I might be pregnant," she reminded him now, though she tried to think of it as little as possible. It was too much to take in. She kept that faintly amused note in her voice. "And we are trapped here, strangers who think the worst of each other. I'll pass on a reprise, thank you."

"This table will do well enough," he continued as if she hadn't spoken, turning so she could see his starkly sensual expression. And that passion in his dark green eyes. Elena's heart gave a hard kick to her ribs, and she felt much too warm, suddenly. "All you need to do is bend over."

The image exploded through her, too vivid, too real. It didn't take much effort at all to imagine him behind her, deep inside her—

"You've obviously had too much to drink," she said. She pressed her napkin to her mouth, more to check that she wasn't trembling than to wipe anything away. She had to stay calm, focused. She had to remember why she was here, why she was doing this.

"Does it make you feel better to think so?" He smiled, and the heat of it catapulted her back to that night in Rome. That dance. The way he'd looked at her, smiled at her, as if she was precious to him. "I haven't. But I want you either way."

She forced a cool smile, and tried to force the past from her head. "You can't have me."

"Why not?" He looked amused, his face carved in those fiercely sensual, powerfully masculine lines, his dark eyes gleaming. Elena fought to restrain her shivery reaction, to ignore that melting, pulling sensation low in her belly. "You've already betrayed your fiancé. What does it matter now how many times you do it?"

She was shocked by how easily he could hurt her, when he should never have had that kind of power in the first place. She should have been pleased that he hated her so openly, that he disdained her so completely. She'd gone out of her way to make sure he did. Instead, it hurt. *It hurt.*

But she couldn't show him that. She could only show him what he wanted to see—what he already saw. A cold, hard woman. Brazen and base.

"I don't like to repeat myself," she said, holding his gaze. "It's boring."

She expected the lash of his temper, but Alessandro laughed. It made the green in his eyes brighten, and worse, made everything inside of her seem to squeeze tight. Breath, belly, core. Even her traitorous heart.

"But you're the one in control, are you not?" he asked, too arrogant, too confident, to believe what he was saying. "Your wish is my command. If you're bored, you need only demand that I relieve it and I will." His smile took on that wolfish edge. "I'm very inventive."

She had a sinking sensation then, as if she'd somehow strayed into quicksand and was moments away from being sucked under. *Think*, she ordered herself in a panic. *Turn this around!*

"And that's all it takes?" She arched her brows high in disbelief. "I need only click my fingers and you'll serve my every whim?"

"Of course." The amusement on his ruthless face did nothing to ease the fierceness of it. And the lie on his lips was laced with laughter. "I am powerless in the face of your machinations, Elena."

Her pulse was wild in her veins, and she felt like prey—like he was stalking her when he hadn't moved. He only stood there, his hands thrust deep in his pockets, and she felt as if she was running hard and scared with his hot breath *right there* on the back of her neck—

"Somehow," she managed to say, her voice cool and dry

rather than panicked, though it cost her, "I have trouble seeing you as *quite* that submissive."

"But this is what you want," he replied in that soft, taunting way, his dark eyes alight. "Isn't that why we're here at all? You demanded it. I obeyed."

Elena had to leave. Now. She had to shut this down before she betrayed herself, before she gave in to the need blazing through her. She would lock herself inside her room, ignore the emptiness and yearning inside of her, and pretend she was locking him out rather than keeping herself in. All she had to do was walk away from him.

She stood in a rush, aware she gave herself away with the speed of it, the total lack of grace. His hard mouth moved into that devastating curve that seemed to curl into the very core of her, making her soften. Ache. She couldn't trust herself to stay, to try to act her way through this. She wanted to run for the door, but she made herself walk instead. As if she was making a simple choice to leave. As if she didn't already feel pursued when he still hadn't moved a muscle.

"I'm not going to chase you through the house, Elena." His voice slid over her, dark and insinuating. Finding its way into her deepest, blackest, most secret corners, far away from any light. Deep into the places she pretended weren't there. "Unless you ask nicely. Is that what you need? Permission to scream *no* at the top of your lungs and know I'll take you, anyway? No responsibility, no regrets?"

The shudder that worked through her then was fierce and deep, involuntary, and she couldn't pretend it had anything to do with revulsion. She felt weak. Weak and desperate. She had to stop walking, had to reach out and hold on to the wall near the wide, arching doorway. She had to fight to keep from revealing how tempted she was, how twisted that made her. She had to keep from confirming what he already seemed to know.

"I don't—" she began desperately, but he sighed impatiently, cutting her off.

"No more lies. Not about this."

Alessandro was leaning back against one of the windows when she turned to look at him again, but nothing about him was languid. She could see his coiled strength, his seething power. He was dressed all in white tonight, and should have looked relaxed. Casual. But he looked more to her like a warrior king, surveying the field of battle and entirely too confident of his own impending victory.

He smiled again, and she felt it bloom inside of her, almost like pain. That low, impossible almost-pain that never entirely left her and that pulsed now, bright and demanding and hungry. Between her legs. In the fullness of her breasts. Even behind her eyes.

"I didn't realize you wanted to play games," she said stiffly, because she had to say something, and she was rapidly forgetting all the reasons why she couldn't simply throw herself at him and worry about it later.

"Of course you did." Laughter lurked in his voice again, gleamed in those dark, knowing eyes. "You want to play them, too."

"I don't." But what if she did? She flushed red hot, imagining.

You are truly shameless, a cold voice hissed inside her, condemning her anew.

Alessandro only crooked his index finger at her then, ordering her to come to him. To admit the things she wanted—to surrender herself to them. To him.

And she wanted that almost more than she could bear.

"No," she said too loudly, and she knew she was talking to herself. To remind herself of who she was, before she did something else she'd bitterly regret.

He wasn't safe, no matter how much that insane part of her insisted otherwise. He wasn't. And she was too afraid that giving in to him, to this, would make her believe she could trust him with the truth. She couldn't.

No matter how hard that was to remember.

"Stop pretending, Elena," he said then, that darker edge in his voice curling around her, drawing her in, calling her out that easily. "You're halfway to desperate. Up all night, tormented and needy. Longing for more but too afraid to ask for it."

That wolf's smile, challenging her. Daring her. Seeing all the things in her she wanted desperately to keep hidden away in the dark. Making her realize that she'd underestimated him, completely. And that he knew that, too.

"I said no," she managed to get out, but her voice was too thick, and it shook, and his smile only deepened.

"I won't even make you beg." He didn't have to do anything but look at her, predatory and sure, and she wanted everything she couldn't have, everything she couldn't risk. She wanted him more than her next breath. "All you have to do is own it. This. Ask and you will receive, *cara.*"

It should have been easy to ignore Alessandro. To shrug off the darkly stirring things he said to her, the fantasies he brought to life within her with so little effort. It should have been simple to concentrate on these weeks of reprieve, and what it meant not to have to look over her shoulder after all these months, not to have to run.

Elena didn't understand why she couldn't seem to do it.

"It's only a matter of time," he'd said in his devastating way that night, when she'd finally turned to go. "Inevitable."

"Nothing is inevitable," she'd bit out over her shoulder, fully aware that he'd been throwing that word back in her face. Remembering exactly when she'd whispered it to him, what she'd felt when she did.

He'd laughed at her. "Keep telling yourself that."

So she did—fervently and repeatedly—but it didn't seem to work.

The nights were long and precarious. Each night she lay awake for hours, trying desperately to think of anything but him, and losing herself in need-infused fantasies instead. Or worse, reliving what had already happened.

Every touch. Every sigh. Every telling whisper.

Even if she managed to fall asleep, there was no relief. She would dream only of him and then wake, heart pounding and mouth dry, her body screaming for his touch. Memories of his possession hot and red in her head, branded into her.

The days were no better. No matter what she did, or where she went in his rambling house or the surrounding grounds, he found her. He was always there. Always watching her with those dark, hungry eyes of his, that wicked smile on his cynical mouth. Always, she understood, a word from her away from catapulting them both straight back into that glorious, terrifying fire that was never quite banked between them.

And all the while, she had to play her role. Cool, sometimes amused, forever teetering on the edge of boredom. The kind of hard, amoral woman Alessandro thought she was. And maybe, she was forced to acknowledge, he wasn't far off.

She could be pregnant—*pregnant*—and all she thought about was the way he'd touched her. While he—the man who might even now be the father of her child—believed she'd sought him out deliberately for sordid reasons of her own, and kept angling to touch her again, anyway. It was appalling. Heartbreaking. Sickening, even. Yet she had no choice but to keep the charade going.

She tried to give him exactly what he expected.

Give him what he wanted, she reasoned, and—assuming she wasn't pregnant, as she had to or she'd go mad—when their time was up he'd send her on her way without another thought, Rome nothing but a distant and dismissed memory. That meant that she would be safe from him and the dark menace of the Corretti family. She was gambling that it also meant he wouldn't bother to use her as any kind of leverage or bartering piece with Niccolo.

But the sick part of her…yearned. No matter what terrible thing came out of her mouth. No matter how much she wished otherwise. It had been hard enough to dance with him, to look at him on that dance floor and *know* him like that. To open up a part of her she'd never known was there, that only he called into being. To feel so safe, so cherished, so perfectly fitted to a complete stranger.

It was worse now. She knew what it was like to have him. She didn't have to *imagine*, she could *remember*. One taste of him wasn't enough. And despite what a mess this all was, despite how much messier it could get if she wasn't careful—she wanted more.

She hated herself for that. It only underscored everything that was wrong with her. Niccolo had been bad enough—but at least he'd fooled her. At least she'd honestly believed he was the man he pretended he was. There was no excuse at all for anything that happened with Alessandro. She'd known better even back in Rome.

She knew better now. But she still couldn't seem to stop.

"Tell me about yourself," he said one night at another long and perilous dinner, his dark voice amused as it so often was. "The story of Elena. We'll endeavor to ignore the sexual tension in the room and you can tell me lies about your idyllic childhood."

"My childhood really was idyllic," she replied, moving her perfectly grilled fish around on her plate.

There was still that part of her that wanted her to tell him everything, to trust him. That part of her that viewed his dark strength as a shelter. He made a sound of disbelief, snapping her out of that same old internal battle.

"It was," she said. "I was loved. I was happy."

He stared at her as if he couldn't make sense of her words, and something twisted inside of her. If he was this thrown by the idea of a happy childhood, it spoke volumes about his own, didn't it? *Don't make him into some kind of misunderstood hero*, she cautioned herself. *He's not one.*

And yet her voice was softer when she continued.

"My parents are good people," she said. It killed her that she had let them down so badly. That she might let them down still further. That she couldn't answer her mother's carefully uncritical emails asking when she'd come home the way she should. It made her want to cry, as usual, and she nearly did. "It was a good life."

"Yet not quite good enough," he said cynically. "You took to Niccolo Falco's version of the high life with alacrity."

"You have no idea what you're talking about," Elena replied, trying to keep the bite from her voice. Though she knew she couldn't defend herself. Not the way she wanted. And certainly not with the truth.

"Money, cars, houses and jewels," he taunted her, as he had long ago. "They make the transition to the ballrooms of Rome feel a great deal smoother, I imagine." His cynical mouth quirked in one corner. "All you have to do is sell your soul, isn't that right?"

"I'm tired of talking about Niccolo," she said, because

she couldn't argue with him without giving herself away, and the fact that she still wanted to explain this to him, that she still so desperately wanted him to know who she really was, horrified her. She eyed him. "What about you?"

"My childhood was significantly less idyllic."

He might as well have been an unyielding, forbidding wall as he gazed back at her. And yet she felt that twist inside of her again.

That poor child, she thought, unable to keep herself from it. *Growing up with those people.*

His eyes narrowed as if he could sense her softening.

"Have we covered enough ground?" he asked, the hint of impatience in his voice, his gaze. "Are you ready to stop playing this game?" His eyes were so dark, so knowing. "I beg of you," he whispered. But he wasn't really begging. He wasn't a man who begged. "Say the word."

But she couldn't let herself do that. She might trust him on some primitive level that defied all reason, that she didn't even understand—but she didn't trust herself. It was much too risky. She shook her head slowly, not looking away from him.

"Don't tell me this is your version of misplaced loyalty," he said, his dark gaze moving over her face. "Once was business, but twice is a betrayal of your beloved Niccolo?"

"Business?" she asked in confusion, but then she remembered. She sighed. "Yes, because I'm spying on you. Over decadent gourmet meals. So far the only thing I've discovered, Alessandro, is that you employ a fantastic chef."

He shook his head, as if she'd disappointed him. "He doesn't deserve your loyalty. He never did."

"Enough about Niccolo," she said, pretending she didn't feel his disappointment like a blow. Pretending she wasn't clamoring to share everything with this man who was wise enough to hate Niccolo. She forced a smile, aware that it was brittle. "Why don't we talk about your fiancée, for a change?"

"What about her?" he asked, as if he'd forgot he ever had a fiancée in the first place. He laughed. "She's hardly worth mentioning. In truth, she never was."

CHAPTER FIVE

"What a lovely sentiment," Elena said dryly. "No wonder she left you."

Something desolate moved over his face then, though he hid it almost the very second she saw it. The lump in her throat stayed where it was.

I hate this, she thought furiously. *I hate* me *like this.*

"Alessia Battaglia had exactly one promise to keep," Alessandro said, no sign of any desolation whatsoever in his hard voice, as if she'd imagined it. "Only one. And she not only failed to keep it, she did so in the most public way possible—designed, I can only assume, to cause me the maximum amount of embarrassment professionally and personally. Which she achieved." His lips twitched. "What is worth mentioning about that?"

"Sometimes people fall out of love," she offered. She was such a fool. She wanted that bleakness she'd seen in his eyes to mean something. His dark green gaze was contemplative as he studied her, and it took everything she had not to look away.

"It was a business arrangement, Elena. Love had nothing to do with it."

An odd sensation worked its way through her then, blooming up from the darkest part of her and uncurling, and it took her long moments to understand that it was a fierce, unwarranted satisfaction. As if the fact he had not loved his fiancée, did not care that she'd left him as much as the fact he'd been left, was not more evidence that he was the worst kind of man—but instead something to celebrate. She despaired of herself.

"And you're surprised she changed her mind?" she asked. That strange feeling hummed in her, making it hard to sit still, to keep her voice so smooth. "Why would anyone subject themselves to an arranged marriage in this day and age? That sounds like the perfect recipe for a lifetime of misery."

"As opposed to what?" He laughed. "The great benefits romance brings to the equation? The jealousy, the emotional manipulation, the very real possibility that at any moment, as you say, people could fall out of it? What makes you think that's the kind of security rational people should build a life on?"

"Because if it's not entirely rational, at least it's honest," she blurted out before she could think better of it. "It's real."

"So is a contract." His voice was dry. Amused. "Which has the added benefit of being tangible. Inarguably rational. And enforceable by law."

"Maybe you were no more than collateral damage." Elena didn't know why she couldn't stop. Why did she care why this man's fiancée had abandoned him? He was Alessandro Corretti. Surely that was reason enough for anyone. "Maybe it wasn't about you at all."

"I was the only one standing at the altar," he said, tilting his head slightly as he gazed at her. "Do you imagine she objected to the priest her father chose? Palermo's great basilica itself? Hundreds of her closest friends and family members?"

"Maybe—" Elena began.

"I don't want to speculate about Alessia Battaglia's tangled, self-serving motives," he said impatiently. "All that matters are her actions. If you want to psychoanalyze a doomed engagement, why not focus on your own?"

"I don't want to talk about Niccolo again." Or that doom he mentioned. Especially not that.

"Then let's talk about you." He lounged there so casually, but Elena knew better. He was still picking at her resistance, over platters of grilled fish and bottles of wine. Over flickering candles and glistening crystal glasses. Over her own objections. "Since you won't let me do what I want to do."

She could almost hear the music they'd danced to, lilting somewhere inside of her. Back when he had looked at her as if she was miraculous, not a battle to be won. Back when he had held her close for such a little while and made her name into a song.

"Fine," she said. Anything to stop the memories, the emotions, that threatened to break her. The lump in her throat returned, and she had to breathe past it. "What do you want to know?"

"The man is a toad." Flat. Certain. Daring her to argue with his characterization. She didn't. "Less than a toad. Yet you agreed to marry him, and for all your faults of character, you don't strike me as the kind of woman you would have to be to overlook such things." Alessandro shifted in his chair, looking even more relaxed, but Elena knew better. She could sense what roared there beneath his skin, powerful and predatory. She could feel it. "Why did you?"

"Because I love—" She caught herself. Barely. She'd almost said *loved.* "I love him." She watched his eyes flash, and enjoyed the fact he didn't like hearing that any more than she liked saying it. "And not because he drove a pretty car or promised me a villa somewhere." She held his gaze, and told the truth. "He was sweet."

"Sweet." Alessandro looked appalled.

"He told me that once he'd seen me, his life could never be the same," she said, letting herself remember when Niccolo had been no more than a handsome, smiling stranger on an otherwise wholly familiar street. "He brought me flowers he picked himself from the hills above the village. He begged me to let him take me to dinner, or even simply take a walk with him near the water. It was the easiest thing in the world to fall for him. He was— He's the most romantic man I've ever met."

"It sounds like a con."

It wasn't as if she didn't agree, but she couldn't show him that. Or admit how ashamed she was of herself for falling for it, head over heels, so easily. Like the little fish she supposed she had been, reeled right into Niccolo's net.

She sniffed. "Says the man who thinks a chilly business contract is a solid basis for a marriage."

"But I am not a toad," he pointed out, dark amusement lurking in his gaze, in the corner of his mouth. "And she did not agree to marry me because I was *sweet.* She agreed to marry me because her father wished it, and because the life I would have given her was generous and comfortable." Again, a lift of those sardonic brows. "That is called practicality. Our situations are not at all similar."

"True." She aimed her smile at him. "But I don't expect Niccolo will leave me at the altar, either."

He stared at her for a long moment, that dark gaze baleful. She shivered, the intensity emanating from him sliding over her skin like a kind of breeze, kicking up goose bumps, though she tried to hide it. Then, not taking his eyes from hers, he threw his napkin on the table and rose.

Liquid and graceful. Powerful and male.

Elena ordered herself to run. But she couldn't seem to move.

Alessandro rounded the table, and then he was behind her, and she thought the heat that exploded through her then might kill her. It hurt when she breathed. It hurt when she held it instead. His hands came down to rest on her shoulders, light and something like innocuous, so nearly polite, and yet she was sure that he could feel the heat of her skin. The bright hot flame she became whenever he touched her.

Remember—an urgent voice cried, deep inside her. *Remember*—

But he was touching her again, he was finally touching her, and she couldn't hold on to a single thought but that.

"Fall for me, then," he said, bending down to speak softly into her ear, his breath tickling her even as it triggered that volcanic need she'd tried too hard to deny. "I'll pick you flowers from the meadow if that's all it takes."

"Stop it," she said, but her voice was so insubstantial. Little more than a whisper, and she knew it told him exactly how affected she was. How little resistance she had left.

"I'll lay you down beneath the moon," he continued as if she hadn't spoken, one clever hand moving beneath her hair to caress the sensitive skin at her nape, and she couldn't contain her shiver then—couldn't hide it from him. "And I'll demonstrate the only kind of love that isn't a sentimental story. The only kind that's real."

He meant sex. She knew he meant sex. And still, *that word.*

That word with his hands on her. *That word* in his low voice, wreaking its havoc as it sunk its claws into her. As it left deep marks that made a mockery of every lie she'd told herself since he'd found her on that boat. Every lie she'd told herself so desperately since that fateful night in Rome.

"I promise you, Elena," he said then, quoting Niccolo, wielding those same words like his own weapon—and a far more deadly one. "Your life will never be the same."

Her heart slammed against her ribs, so hard she worried they might crack. Once. Then again. Elena was lost. Held securely in his hands and unable to think of a single reason why she should extricate herself. Why she should do anything at all but let herself fall into this magnificent fire and burn herself away until there was nothing left of her but smoke. And him.

His hands dropped to her chair to pull her back from the table, and by the time she stood on her trembling legs, by the time she turned to look at his beautiful face made no less arrogant by the heat stamped across it, she remembered. If not herself, not entirely, than some tiny little spark of self-preservation that reminded her what was at stake. What there was left to lose.

His clever eyes moved over her face, and he frowned, reaching out again to take her upper arms in his hands. His thumbs moved over the skin the sleeveless empire-cut top she wore left bare, sending his personal brand of electricity arrowing straight into her core.

Where she ached. And melted. And ached anew.

"Don't," he said, urgency making his voice harsh. "Don't walk away again."

"I have to," she replied, but she couldn't look away from him. She couldn't move.

"There's no one on this island but you and me and the people I pay exorbitantly to keep my secrets," he said, all temptation and demand, and she could feel him, feel *this*, feel the dizzying intensity in every cell of her body. In every breath. In the way her heart beat and her pulse pounded. "No one to see what you do. No one to know. No one to contradict you if you lie about it later."

"I'll know," she said quietly.

And knew immediately, when his expression changed, that she'd made a critical mistake. For a moment she didn't understand, though the air between them seemed to burst into flames. His face lit with a dark, almost savage triumph, and his hard mouth curved.

"Yet we both know where your moral compass points, don't we?"

"Away from you," she said hurriedly, but it was too late.

"Another lie is as good a word as any, Elena," he said then, more wolf in that moment than man. "I accept."

Alessandro pulled her to him with that ruthless command that undid her—that thrilled her no matter how she wished it didn't. And her body simply obeyed. She knew she should resist this. She knew she needed to push him away, to wrench herself out of his arms before—

But she didn't.

She didn't even try.

He took her mouth, masterful and merciless at once, inevitable, and Elena melted against him, went up on her toes, and met him.

Finally.

His mouth was on her again, at last, and it wasn't enough. Her taste flooded him, driving him wild. Her tongue was an exquisite torture against his, her head tilting at the slightest touch of his hand for that perfect, slick fit he craved. He pulled her even closer, bending her back over his arm, kissing her as if both their lives depended on it.

Mine, he thought, with a ferocity that shook through him and only made him want her that much more.

She was pliant and beautiful, graceful in his arms, her luscious body plastered against him. He could feel her breasts against his chest, her hips pressed to his, and he was fervently grateful she was the sort of woman who wore shoes with wicked heels so gracefully. It made it that much easier to haul the delectable place where her legs met against the hardest part of him, right where he wanted her.

God, how he wanted her.

He lost his head. He forgot what he'd planned, what he'd intended here—he tasted her and the whole world fell away, narrowed down to one specific goal. To thrust himself inside her, again and again. To make them both shatter into a thousand pieces.

To take them both home.

He reached down and pulled her black top up over those fantastic breasts she never covered with any kind of bra, muttering words he hardly understood in Sicilian as well as Italian. He ran his fingers over her taut nipples, watched her bite her lip against the pleasure of it, her head falling back to give him better access.

But it wasn't enough, so he backed her up against the table and set her there, leaning down to lick his way from one delicious crest to the other. To lose himself in the softness of her warm skin, the scent of it, and those small, high cries she made when he took a nipple deep into his mouth.

She was gripping the edge of the table, her breath coming in hard, quick bursts, and she was so beautiful he thought he might die if he couldn't bury himself in her. If he couldn't feel her tremble all around him, screaming out his name. If he couldn't drive so deep into her he'd forget all about who he'd once imagined she was. Who she should have been.

Who she wasn't, damn her.

He remembered the stark, sensual picture he'd drawn for her at that dinner weeks back and smiled then, against the delicate skin beneath one of her breasts. He straightened, tugged her to her feet and found himself distracted by the glaze of passion in her bright summer eyes, the color high on her cheeks. He held her face between his hands, his thumbs sweeping from her temples to those elegant cheekbones that drove him mad, and plundered her mouth.

Taking, tasting. Exulting in this, in her. Making her his the only way he could.

He tore his mouth from hers, then spun her around. He felt her tremble against him as he leaned her forward, spreading her before him over the table, using one hand to push a forgotten serving dish, piled high with the remains of fluffy, fragrant rice, out of her way.

"Alessandro…" she whispered as she bent there, offering him the perfect, delectable view. A prayer. A vow. So much more than simply his name.

He smoothed his hands down her back, the sensual shape of her making him harder, making him desperate. But he didn't rush. He reached around beneath her to flatten his hands against the delectable curve of her belly.

He held his hands there for a moment, savoring the fine, low tremor that shuddered through her. Letting her absorb the heat of his hands. And then he moved lower, pulling open the button fly of her trousers with one hand as the other slid inside to cup her scalding heat in his palm.

She was panting now, leaning her forehead against the table, and he held her femininity in his hand, hot and damp and swollen with desire. And then he squeezed.

Elena bucked against him, against the table, and he did it again. Then again.

Slowly, deliberately, he built up a rhythm. Teasing her. Seducing her. Pressing against her urgent center with every stroke. Her breath grew ragged, her heat bloomed into his hand, and only then—only when she was mindless before him, stretched out breathless and boneless and his to command—did he pull his hand away.

Leaving her trembling right there on the edge.

She sobbed something incoherent into the arm she had thrown up near her head and then let out a moan as Alessandro tugged on her trousers, peeling them over her hips and shoving them down her legs to her knees. He left her panties where they were, an electric blue thong that beautifully framed then disappeared between the perfect twin curves of her pert bottom.

She was restless, shifting her weight from one foot in its high wedged sandal to the other, her hips swaying in an age-old invitation that speared into him like a new heat, mesmerizing him for a moment. Her shoes lifted her to him, making her arch her back slightly as she sprawled there before him, mindless and moaning. His in every way.

He loved it. He thought he could die in this moment a happy man at last, this woman his own, perfectly crafted feast—and he intended to eat every bite. He traced over her thong with a lazy finger, then ran his hands over her bottom, vowing that one day he would learn every millimeter of her with his mouth. Every hollow. Every mark. With his teeth. His tongue.

But not now. His need was like a wild storm in him, pounding in his blood, making his chest tight and his vision narrow.

He freed himself from his trousers and quickly rolled on the protection he'd carried in his pocket, then bent over her, shoving her thong down and out of his way. She was still trembling, still breathing hard and fast, and her eyes were shut tight. He braced himself on one arm, his hand flat against the table near her shoulder.

"Alessandro," she said again, her voice strangled, but she lifted her hips when he slid a hand beneath her, pressing her face against the table as if it was a pillow.

He reached down and pressed hard against her center even as he shifted his position and drove straight into her.

She came apart beneath him, sobbing and wild.

He had to grit his teeth as she shuddered, as her fingers pressed into the table's hard surface as if she could find some hold. He let her ride it out, waiting hot and hard and deep inside of her, her perfect bottom snug against him, almost more enticement than he could bear.

When she started to come back to him, he began to move.

He wasn't gentle. She made that small, highly aroused noise in the back of her throat, the sweetest sound he'd ever heard, and met him, thrust for thrust. She was sinuous and lithe, arched there before him with her black top flowing all around her as she moved with him, like some kind of erotic dance.

It was almost too much for him. He reached out and held the nape of her neck in his hand, making her shudder, then keeping her still.

And then he simply took her.

He ravaged. He savored. *He took.*

And all the while she cried out her pleasure, her hips wild against his, her eyes shut tight and her cheeks stained red with all of that desperate, delicious heat.

It was perfect. She was perfect.

"You are mine," he ground out from between his teeth, his hips hard against hers, riding her, devouring her. *"Mine."*

When he couldn't hold on any longer he slid a hand beneath her once more, finding the heart of her hunger and rubbing hard against it, making her jerk against him.

"Again," he ordered her, his voice so deep, so guttural, he hardly recognized it. And he didn't care, his own climax roaring toward him. "Now."

She obeyed him with a beautiful scream, her feet leaving the ground as she shattered into a flare of white hot heat around him, catapulting over that edge once more.

And finally, *finally,* he followed.

Alessandro didn't know how long it was before he caught his breath. Before he was himself again, and not just a handful of scattered fragments thrown to every corner of this island. Of the globe.

Elena still lay beneath him, her cheek pressed against the tabletop, and he could feel every breath she took. He angled himself back and off her, regretting that he had to pull out of her soft heat.

She didn't move, or open her eyes. Alessandro rid himself of the protection he'd used, fastened his trousers, and still she lay there. Making a perfectly debauched, impossibly lovely picture. Her trousers and thong were a tangle at her knees, her sweet bottom and the feminine secrets beneath on display as she bent there over his table so obediently, her mouth slightly ajar as she breathed and her slender arms thrown out before her as if in total surrender.

Desire coiled within him again, and he rubbed his hands over his face as if that might make sense of this hunger. Nothing eased it. Not even the one thing that should have.

He wondered, then, if it would ever leave him. If he would ever be free of it. Of her.

Is that what you want? a voice queried from a place inside of him he preferred to ignore, and he shoved it away.

"Elena."

She stirred then, her eyes fluttering open, and Alessandro watched as she slowly peeled herself up from the table, then reached down to pull her panties and her trousers into place, all without looking his way. All a bit shaky, a bit too careful, as if she wasn't sure her legs would hold beneath her. Her hair was a wanton tangle around her face but she ignored it, not even pushing it out of her way as she buttoned up her denim trousers.

So he did it for her, tucking a silken blond sheaf behind one ear.

"Are you all right?"

Her gaze flicked to his, then away.

"Yes," she said. Her voice was rough and she coughed. "Of course."

But there was a defenseless cast to her jaw as she said it, and he reached over to tilt up her chin, forcing her to look at him. Her blue eyes were stormy, and there was something somehow bruised about the way she stared back at him. He felt cold.

"Are you?" he asked again, his tone serious. Gruff.

She knocked his hand away. He let her.

"Please don't patronize me." She looked around as if in search of something, but only hugged herself instead. As if, he thought, she was very small. The cold in him grew wider, deeper. "I said I was fine."

He studied her, battling the strangest urge to pull her into his arms, to hold her against him. To warm them both. It was ridiculous.

And then he did it anyway, not understanding himself at all.

She fit beneath his chin and securely against his chest, and he couldn't have said what he felt then. It didn't make sense. He didn't recognize it—or himself. And yet he held her, he listened to her breathe, and he hated it when she pulled away from him.

"Stop this," she said in a low voice, her gaze dark and troubled. "I don't need your backhanded form of comfort."

He didn't understand any of this. Why was he having this conversation in the first place? He didn't tolerate scenes like this. He avoided even the faintest hint of what he saw swimming there in all of that summer blue. So why was he still standing here?

"Elena," he began.

She blew out a breath. "I asked you to stop," she whispered.

Alessandro felt profoundly off balance. Uneven down into his soul. He scowled.

"So I can take you any way I please," he said in a less pleasant voice than he might have, had he been able to make this strange feeling disappear. Had any of this made sense to him. "I can bend you over a table and make you scream and shake, and you'll submit to that happily. Greedily."

Her face paled, but that didn't stop him. And whatever was happening inside of him shifted, turned furious. At himself, at her—he couldn't tell the difference. He just needed this feeling to stop. Now.

"There is nothing I couldn't make you beg me to do to you, is there?" He folded his arms across his chest. "Nothing at all."

"Does this make you feel better?" she asked, lifting her head, her eyes flashing.

"I'm not the one who has convenient pretensions of modesty, Elena," he bit out. "But only when it suits."

He watched her shake that off, a quick jerk of her smooth shoulders, and wondered that it even hurt her.

"I know you don't respect me, Alessandro," she said, and her voice wasn't angry. It was something else. Something that worked in him like shame, oily and thick. "I know exactly what you think of me. You've told me repeatedly. You don't have to act it out again now."

"You don't respect yourself!" he threw at her. How did she dare?

"But you should." She shook her head, then he saw to his horror that her eyes were full. Though she didn't cry. She only looked at him with tears bright in her gaze and he felt small. Mean. "Shouldn't you? What kind of man does the things you do with me, revels in them, and yet has no respect for me at all?"

"Elena," he began, but there was too much inside of him. It was too big and too dangerously unwieldy, and it had something to do with that way she looked at him. As if she thought he was a better man. That he ought at least to try. And that vulnerability in the way she held herself, as if she knew what he'd long suspected—that, deep down, he wasn't. And never had been.

"You call me a whore and then you call me yours," she said quietly. "Am I the one who doesn't respect myself or is that you?"

He felt buffeted by wild, treacherous storms—but yet he stood still, and there was only that way she gazed at him, as if she saw through all of his darkness and saw what lay there on the other side of it. Something he refused to name.

Something that could not exist. He wouldn't allow it.

"It's like you're two different women," he told her when he was sure he could keep his balance. When he'd beat back the storms as best he could. "One I know all too well. One who would marry a man like Niccolo Falco and defend that choice, call it romantic."

She looked away from him then. In shame? In some kind of triumph that he cared this much, so much more than he should, than he even admitted to himself?

How could he still not know?

"But the other, Elena." He dropped his voice, and saw her eyes close against it, as if it tempted her beyond endurance, or hurt her. As if he did. "The other…"

Was the woman he'd imagined she was when he'd met

her. The woman he'd wanted so desperately he'd ignored her association with Niccolo to dance with her, to hold her. The woman he'd called his before he knew her name. The woman he sometimes saw in her still—like now....

That woman doesn't exist, he reminded himself harshly. She hadn't then and she never would.

"People are complicated," she said after a moment, a bleakness making her blue gaze gray when she looked at him again. "You can't shove them into little boxes. And you can't really know them unless they let you."

"Or they show you," he agreed. "As you have."

She swallowed, and then her head bowed forward, only slightly, but Alessandro saw it. He knew defeat when it stood before him. That should mean he'd won, that he was victorious in this—whatever this was. It should mean he felt triumph at the very least. And instead what he felt was empty.

"The show's over, Alessandro," she whispered, and he couldn't make sense of what he saw on her face then.

Perhaps because he couldn't, he didn't stop her when she turned and walked away from him, again, leaving him there alone in the quiet room, the echoes of the passion they'd shared seeming to cling to the walls like rich, wild tapestries.

And still he tried to work out what he'd seen on her elegant features before she'd left. Temper, certainly. The lingering trace of that powerful desire that, it seemed, never truly left either one of them. A kind of weary resignation.

And sadness.

It was like a punch to the gut.

Elena was sad. And he'd made her that way.

She had looked at him like he was a monster. Worse, as if she knew he'd chosen to become exactly that. As if she knew he'd vowed he would never become this kind of

man—a man of cruelty and dark impulse like his father—
no matter the provocation, and then had gone ahead and
done it, anyway.

As if she knew.

He wasn't sure he could live with it. He wasn't sure he
could bear being this much of a disappointment to himself, this much of a bastard.

But he didn't know how to stop.

CHAPTER SIX

"I WANT YOU in my bed," he said curtly later that same night, appearing in the doorway of her bedchamber.

Elena was curled up in the blue-and-white armchair near one of the sweeping, open windows, staring out at the dark sea and the silver pathway that rippled there, stretching toward the swollen orange moon hanging low on the horizon. She'd been thinking about resistance. About surrender.

About how to use this uncontrollable passion for her own ends before it swallowed her whole.

"I knew I meant to lock that door," she murmured, dropping her mask into place as she turned to look at him.

"Tonight," Alessandro told her in that same clipped, commanding tone, the slight narrowing of his fierce eyes the only indication he'd heard her. "And for good. This particular game is over and I think we both know you lost."

He'd showered. She could smell the faint scent of his soap, fresh and clean. His thick hair lay in damp waves on his head, and he no longer looked the way he had when she'd left him in the dining room. Bereft, she might have said, if he were a smaller creature, a lesser man.

He expected her to resist him. Still. Again. Elena could see it in the way he held himself, the fine lines of his powerful body taut. She could see it in the way his dark green gaze was hooded, yet tracked her every breath.

So what if you lose a little bit more of yourself? she asked herself briskly, shoving aside what felt like a kind of despair, concentrating instead on that ravenous hunger for him she couldn't seem to escape. That was what she had to exploit. The possibility of a pregnancy had brought her this far—passion would do the rest. It had to. *There are worse things to lose—and far worse fates.*

"All right," she said.

The moment stretched out. He cocked his head slightly to one side, eyes narrow and jaw hard. "What did you say?"

"I'm agreeing with you, Alessandro." She swung her feet off the chair, pressing her bare toes into the polished wood floor beneath her. Like that would keep her grounded. Like anything could. "You win."

There was a tense, shimmering silence. Elena kept her gaze trained down at her bare feet, on the toes she'd painted a bright pink in some attack of hopefulness when she'd still worked on his yacht—but then, she didn't have to look at him to feel the way he was glaring at her. The fire and the force of him like a wild heat against her skin. A dark magic inside of her, changing her. Ruining her.

Only if I let it, she assured herself. She might lose a bit of herself, but it was worth it, wasn't it? She was safe here, and she needed to stay that way. And he would lose interest in her all the quicker once she ceased to be a challenge, because that was how men like him operated—so this would ensure that when their forty days were up, he would wash his hands of her. Discard her, happily, without bothering to inform on her to Niccolo. She would be free, and Niccolo would have lost her trail completely.

This was insurance, plain and simple.

"And what," he asked, his low voice threaded with seductive, sensual menace, "do I win, Elena? Be specific."

She lifted her head. His expression was deeply cynical, his stance tense, and yet that same passion burned in him, bright and hot, as obvious to her as if it was tattooed across his face.

"Whatever you like," she told him.

She raised her brows as he only stood there in the door-way and did no more than continue to study her, as if she was a code he intended to break. A trickle of apprehension worked its way down her spine—because she couldn't let him do that. He could have her, but not all of her. And never the truth.

"Isn't this what you want?" she asked, taunting him. Distracting him. She smiled, cool and challenging. "My complete and total surrender, entirely on your terms? Well, here it is. This is what it looks like. You should be pleased, surely."

"Is that meant to shame me?" he countered, a dark gleam in his eyes then, and Elena had to fight back an involuntary shiver. "I think you'll find I'm far past that. Nothing can. Certainly not you."

"Then you have nothing to fear." She stood, smooth-ing her hands down the front of the silk-and-lace chemise she wore, in a soft champagne shade that she knew made her eyes that much bluer. "I found this on the end of the bed, like all the rest of the clothes I've found waiting for me since I got here. It's as if you make them all yourself in some secret workshop in the night."

"Not me." There was a sardonic curve to his mouth, but his dark eyes burned as he watched her walk toward him. Possessive. Hungry. "My cousin Luca runs a fashion house. We may not be close, but the clothes speak for themselves."

Elena didn't say anything. She wasn't sure she could, now that she was really going through with this. It was one thing to decide to surrender herself to this man, at least in bed. It was something else again to *do* it.

It might very well shred her into tiny little pieces she wasn't sure she'd ever manage to put back together. But she knew this was the only way.

And she couldn't deny the fact that it excited her. That he did. That the idea of sharing his bed made her shiver with need, no matter what price she'd end up paying.

She walked toward him, holding his gaze. Letting her hips sway beneath the silken embrace of the fabric that clung to her. Letting him watch, wait. She could see the stamp of hunger across his face. She could see the blaze of it in his eyes.

And felt more powerful in this moment than she had in a very long time. Since she'd looked up from her life to find a shockingly beautiful man watching her as if she was a goddess come down to earth. She felt it hum in her like an electrical current.

She stopped when she was no more than a breath away and stood there. She waited. He tensed, but he didn't move. His hands were thrust deep into the pockets of his loose black trousers as if he was perfectly at ease, but she knew better.

"Do you think this will work, Elena?" he asked, his voice hoarse. "This suspicious capitulation, this attempt at seduction, coming so soon on the heels of your deep concerns about respect?"

"You should ask yourself," she said, her tone light, though her gaze was hard on his, "why even when I do what you say you want, you accuse me of something. Anything."

"Because it won't," he said, answering his own question. His mouth twisted. "Not the way you imagine. I don't care how you come to me. I don't care how I have you. I don't care at all, so long as I do. Are you prepared for that?"

"I told you," she said softly. "You win." She held out

her arms like some kind of supplicant, but she smiled like a queen. "To the victor go the spoils—isn't that what they say?"

"They do."

He reached over and traced a deceptively lazy trail from the wildly fluttering pulse in her throat to the hollow between her breasts. All of his ruthlessness, all of his simmering power, in that one fingertip.

"You should be afraid of me," he told her then, and his voice moved in her, threat and promise, sex and demand, and something even darker in his eyes. "Why aren't you?"

"I'm terrified," she whispered, but she wasn't. And she could see he knew it.

"I wish I knew which one of us is the greater fool," he replied in the same harsh whisper, and it made her throat constrict.

"Someone once told me you should be careful what you wish for, Alessandro," she said, because it was better to taunt him. It was better to push. Safer. "You just might get it, and then what will you do?"

Her heart beat like a hammer in her chest, in her breasts, between her legs, and she could swear he heard it, too, because his hard mouth curved, not a trace of cynicism to be seen. Only desire.

And that was all the warning she got.

He hauled her up into the air, then threw her over one shoulder like she weighed nothing at all. Like the warrior king she'd imagined him. Claiming her that easily—that completely.

She gasped—but his hand came down on her bottom, his big, hard palm holding her fast and warning her, and she gulped her own words down.

His shoulder was wide and hard against her belly as he moved through the house; his hand was a hot brand of fire against the exposed skin of her behind, the backs of her thighs. She caught a glimpse of herself as they passed a mirror, hanging down his strong back, her hair wild and her face flushed, and it made her breath go shallow. She couldn't stop trembling, and it still wasn't fear.

Surrender, she told herself. *It's the only way to save everything else that matters.* But what scared her wasn't the act of surrendering to him. It was that it was so easy. That it felt so good.

Alessandro tossed her down in the center of his bed, and she had only a quick impression of bold colors, dark woods and arching windows wide open to let the night inside. Then her gaze fixed on him, and stayed put. He stood by the side of the wide bed for a moment, looking down at her as she sprawled there, and she couldn't quite read the intense look in his eyes, on his hard face.

But she trembled. And wanted. And melted into liquid fire.

He didn't ask. He didn't ply her with more of those lethal, sensual promises of his, those half terrifying and half intriguing things he'd said he would do to her, with her, if only she'd ask.

He simply took.

And she gloried in that, too.

This is exactly what you wanted, Elena reminded herself a week or so later as she stood in that gorgeous shower room built outside to take in the sunlight and the crisp sea air.

She tilted her face up into the spray, and let the heat work its way into her as she considered her success. Her delicious, dangerous surrender.

There was no part of her body Alessandro hadn't claimed. No millimeter of skin he hadn't investigated with his fingers, his mouth, his wicked tongue. He took her with a ferocity and a kind of desperation she understood too well, because it was in her, too, this terrible hunger. It was never satisfied. It never dimmed.

No matter how many times he tore her apart, no matter how often she screamed his name and then held him close as he collapsed against her, it was still there. Moving within her. Ripping her open. Making her fear it would be impossible to ever really leave this man, that this kind of hunger would mark her, scar her....

But she'd returned the favor. She'd thrown herself head-first into that fire, and who cared what burned? She'd pushed him down on that same dinner table and climbed on top of him, using her mouth and hands to make him groan. She'd learned what made him burst into flame, what made him roll her over and take control, what made him laugh in the dark as they explored each other. She'd teased him, taken him, taunted him—and then slept wrapped up against him, held close against that powerful chest of his, lulled into sleep by the steady beat of his heart.

This is what success feels like, she told herself now. *You should be happy.* But instead, she pictured them dancing, around and around in that ballroom, all of that wonder and delight between them. It glowed in her still, even here. Even now.

What they could have been. What they should have been.

She shouldn't let herself dream about such things, because it only hurt her. She shouldn't let herself imagine what it would be like if none of what had happened on this island had that darker undertone, if this wasn't one more game they played. If it really meant something when he kissed her face and smiled at her, when she held him close and whispered his name.

If it meant what she'd seen back then, glimmering between them, just out of reach—

Snap out of the daydream, she ordered herself now, annoyed at herself and that gnawing ache in her chest that made her feel so hollow. *You're here to be the whore he thinks you are. Nothing more.*

It turned out, she was good at that.

She shut off the water and reached for her towel, and he was there when she opened her eyes. Her stomach still clenched. Her heart still jumped. He was still so impossibly beautiful, fierce and male, standing in the open door between his suite and the open shower area, his arms crossed over his bare chest.

"How long have you been there?" she asked. She had to fight to make her voice smooth, and she didn't know why. It should have been easy after all this practice. It should have been second nature by now.

"Not long."

"Weren't you going for a run?"

"I was." He smiled. "I did."

"I must have spent more time in the shower than I realized."

She wanted to sound light. Easy. She couldn't understand why that raw, hollow place inside of her still bled into everything. As if it mattered how close this all was to what it should have been, yet wasn't.

And won't ever be, she reminded herself.

"Do you think you're pregnant?" he'd asked one afternoon, the sun pouring in through the windows, bathing them both in white light as they moved together on his bed. He'd run his hands over her belly, his gentle touch at distinct odds with his gruff voice. It had been too much. There'd been that look in his eyes, so close to a kind of yearning. It had torn her up inside.

She'd been straddling him, and she'd twisted her hips to take him deep inside of her. Sex was better than emotion. Easier. He'd hissed out a breath, his dark eyes narrowing.

"We'll find out soon enough," she'd said, reminding him who they were, moving against him to make her point. "And then we can stop pretending there's anything more to this than sex."

He'd reached up to pull her mouth down to his, and he'd whispered something against her lips. It had only been later, when they'd collapsed again, breathless and destroyed, that she'd realized what he'd said. *Damn you.*

She walked toward him now, wrapping the towel around her, and he stepped back to let her pass. She made her way into his bedroom and over toward the massive bed that dominated the far wall, angled for the best view out of the many windows.

None of this was what she'd thought it would be. He wasn't the man she'd believed he was. He was nothing like Niccolo, and she didn't know how to process that. She'd expected the fire to dissipate the more she indulged herself in him, showing her what horrors lay beneath. But Alessandro wasn't made of Niccolo's brand of bright surface charm to hide the bully within, or if he was, he was better at concealing it. He was gruff and hard, ruthless and demanding—but he was also surprisingly thoughtful. Caring in ways that made it hard for her to breathe, much less throw out the next, necessary barb. As likely to take the hairbrush from her hand and brush her hair, making her tremble with something far different from lust when he met her eyes in the mirror, as he was to throw her up against the nearest wall and let the raging fire consume them.

He's like Niccolo. He's worse than Niccolo. She chanted it at herself. *You might not be able to see it, but it's there. It has to be there.*

Because if he wasn't like Niccolo, if she'd been that terribly wrong about him, then she had no reason not to trust him the way she wished she could. She might feel oddly safe with him, still. He might thrill her in ways she was afraid to admit to herself. But she'd been running for too long, and there was as much to lose now as there had been when she'd started.

More, perhaps, if she counted her foolish heart, and the way it beat for him.

"What's the matter?" he asked from behind her, that combination of perception and kindness in his tone that was uniquely his. It undid her.

But she couldn't cry. She couldn't betray herself like this, when she'd come so far and given up so much.

Elena turned to face him. She met his dark gaze, saw the concern there that she couldn't acknowledge, that she couldn't let herself accept. Alessandro's mouth crooked in one corner, and that was all it took for her to melt. To want. To topple over into that stark, demanding need.

"Come here," she said, her voice husky with the things she couldn't say, the truths she couldn't tell.

And he obeyed, this fierce predator of a man, his dark eyes bright and fixed on her with that same hunger. She waited until he was close and then she dropped the towel, and he laughed.

"You'll be the death of me," he said in that low voice that made her skin prickle, and then his hands were on her skin, lifting her and pushing her back onto the bed, coming down on top of her with that delicious weight of his, smooth muscle and dangerous man.

"I'll sing the elegy at your funeral," she promised him, and his smile deepened in a way that made her ache everywhere, hot and greedy for him.

"I won't die alone." He buried his hands in her wet

hair, pulling her mouth to within a breath of his. "I promise you that."

Their gazes tangled, held, as she reached between them and pulled him free from his running shorts. As she reached for the side table, then rolled protection down over the hard, smooth length of him. As she guided him to her entrance.

"Elena," he whispered. "I—"

But words were even more dangerous than he was. She couldn't have it. She couldn't risk it. She moved her hips against him, inviting him in. Making him groan. Keeping him quiet.

Being the whore he thought she was, or she thought she was, or this situation had made her. She told herself it didn't matter anymore. She only knew she had to see it through.

He pushed inside of her, and they both sighed. That perfect, impossible fit. That slick, wild fire. That coil of desire, tight and hot, that only seemed stronger every time.

This was killing them, she thought then, her gaze locked to his, lost in his, truths shimmering between them that she refused to voice. He knew things he shouldn't know, the way he always had, and they might as well be dancing still, around and around, as familiar and as lost to each other as ever.

But he moved in her then, commanding and powerful and hers—hers despite everything as he had been from that first glance, that very first touch of their hands—and she forgot again, the way she always did.

For a little while.

Alessandro stalked out of the house.

He moved across the terrace toward the pool, where Elena sat on one of the loungers, whiling away another summer morning. She looked perfectly at ease, while he was still boiling over with all the frustration he'd unloaded on his assistant over the past few hours. He made a mental note to increase the man's annual bonus.

"One more week, Giovanni," he'd snapped when yet another Corretti family crisis had been trotted out as if it was a critical business issue that required his immediate attention. Because Alessandro was expected to care, to be responsible. To handle everyone else's mess. "I'm on holiday. Tell them to sort it out themselves, or wait."

"But, sir..." His assistant had cleared his throat. "They grow more insistent by the hour!"

"Then I suggest you earn your outrageous salary," Alessandro had growled, ending the call. But it hadn't done much for the restless agitation that still coursed through him, making him feel edgy.

He slowed as he drew closer to Elena, tucked up in the shade of an umbrella, paging through foreign magazines with every outward appearance of lazy contentment. For some reason, that flipped a kind of switch in him.

One more week to forty days. One more week until he and Elena were finished—or bound together in a way he'd tried not to think about too closely. One more week, and he wasn't ready.

He didn't want the life he'd left behind when he'd fled Sicily a month ago. He didn't want to slip back into that same old role that had brought him nothing but grief for the whole of his adult life. He didn't want to dance to the tune of a dead man, or fight these losing battles against his family's bad reputation. He was as tired of it as he'd been the day he'd left.

Just as he was fed up with Elena's stubborn determination to keep him at arm's length.

He knew what she was doing, with her mysterious smiles and the sex she doled out as if she was nothing more than a sensual buffet and he a mindless glutton. She was giving him what she thought he wanted. Soothing the savage beast.

But he knew there was more to her, and he wanted it. He was so damned tired of half measures, of *almost*. He wanted everything she had. Every last secret. He wanted to know her better than he knew himself.

He wanted *her*.

Alessandro was sick and tired of settling for less.

"It's been thirty-three days, Elena," he said when he reached her side. He waited until she looked up from her magazine, and then smiled. "Does that mean we already have our answer?"

"Good morning to you, too," she said in her usual way, arch and arid, but this time he sensed her temper beneath it. And he couldn't have said why he wanted to see it so much, so badly. "And no. There are a few days left before I'd jump to any conclusions."

For a moment, they only gazed at each other, and he could feel what flowed between them. That wild electricity, as always, but there was something else beneath it. Something real. He was sure of it.

She shifted position, and smiled in a way she knew by now was guaranteed to poke at his hunger. Her fingers plucked at the ragged hem of the denim shorts she wore beneath an open-necked, nearly sheer shirt that flowed all around her in bright reds and deep blues, hinting at the delectable curves beneath. Her smooth legs went on forever, sun-kissed and shaped so beautifully. She patted the lounger beside her, and it caused him physical pain not to put his hands on her. Not to wrap those legs around his waist, throw them over his shoulders, revel in all the ways he wanted her.

But it wasn't enough, and he didn't care that she wanted

it that way. That she was using their explosive chemistry to hide in. He couldn't allow it any longer.

"I wonder what would happen if we kept our clothes on," he said then, quietly, and her eyes widened. "What then, Elena? What do you think we'd discover?"

"That we are perfect strangers," she replied coolly, but her clear eyes darkened. "Who never should have met in the first place."

"I'm not convinced." He held her gaze, saw the hint of panic in hers. "What are you hiding?"

He was sure he saw her flinch, then control it. Almost too fast to track.

"What could I possibly be hiding?" she retorted. "You've taken everything. You know everything. There's nothing left."

"I've taken your body, yes," he agreed. "I know it very well, just as you intended. But what about the rest of you?"

He watched her struggle, one emotion after the next moving across her face, and he knew he was right. She shook her head, her blue eyes cloudy.

"What do you care?" she asked quietly. "You have what you want."

"I want everything," he said, raw and intense, and smiled when she jerked back against the lounger.

And everything might not be enough, a voice whispered deep inside of him. He might have been a ruined thing, twisted and dark all the way through, but he needed this. He needed her. He didn't care why. He only knew he did.

He watched her pull in a breath, then another, and she curled her hands into tight fists on her thighs. He forced himself to wait. She looked away for a long, tense moment, and when her eyes met his again, he saw her. *Her.*

At last.

"I knew it," he said with deep satisfaction. "I knew you were right there, simmering beneath the surface."

"What do you want, Alessandro?" she asked, and her voice was neither cool nor amused, for the first time in a very long while. "We only have a few days left here. Why ruin them with this?"

"I want the woman I met in Rome," he told her. "I don't want a damned sex toy."

She let out a short, derisive laugh. "Of course you do. Men like you always do."

He felt that same familiar darkness in him expanding, rising, sweeping through him, reminding him how ruined and twisted he was and always had been, since the day he was born. *Men like you.* Would he never escape his name? Was he doomed to be exactly like his father, no matter how hard he'd struggled against it?

"I don't care if you hate me, Elena," he gritted out. "But whatever else this is, whatever happens, I want it to be real."

Because one thing in his life had to be. Just one thing.

"'Real,'" she repeated in a flat tone. "You. That's almost funny. What do you know about *real*?" Her face heated as she spoke, her temper flooding in like a rising tide and as beautiful to him, however perverse that was. "You almost married a woman for what? A business expense?"

"Duty," Alessandro corrected her, and she laughed.
She laughed.

"The reality, Alessandro, is that you are not a good man," she said with an awful, deliberate finality, staring straight at him, deliberate and pointed. "How could you be? You're a Corretti."

Condemnation and curse, all wrapped up in his name. His damned name. She said it as if it was the vilest word imaginable. As if the very saying of it blackened her tongue. He felt something crack open inside of him.

Because, of course, he wasn't simply a Corretti. He was the one his family was happy to sacrifice to serve their own ends. He was the one who was expected to do his duty, because he always had. His own parents had used him as a pawn. His grandfather had manipulated him. His "business expense" had walked out on him. Then Elena had crashed into his life like a lightning bolt, illuminating all of his darkest corners in that single, searing, impossible dance, but she hated him—he'd made sure of it. He had never been anything but a dark, ruined thing, masquerading as a man.

"Your conscience will be your undoing, boy," Carlo had jeered at him more than once. "It makes you weak."

As long as it didn't make him Carlo, he thought now, bitterly. Perhaps that was the most he could hope for.

Elena had no clue what she was dealing with. No possible clue what he held in check. "You don't have the slightest idea who I am."

"The entire world knows who you are," she retorted, glaring at him as if he'd never been anything but a monster, and he couldn't stand it. Not any longer. Not from her. "You're—"

"I am so tired of paying for the sins of others," he gritted out. He slashed a hand through the air when she opened her mouth and she shut it again, sinking back against the lounger, her hands in fists at her sides. "I've spent my life doing nothing but the right thing, and it still doesn't matter. Yes, I was going to marry that girl." He raked a hand through his hair. "Because it was my grandfather's dying wish and I am many things, Elena, none of them as polluted or as vile as you seem to believe, but I could not defy my own grandfather."

"Your grandfather—" she began, her eyes flashing, and he knew what she was about to say. The stories she was about to tell. His twisted family history in all its corrupt glory.

"Was no saint," he interrupted her. "I know. But he was my *grandfather,* Elena, and whatever else I might think of the way he lived his life, I have him to thank for mine. How do you repay that kind of debt?"

"Selling yourself off to the highest bidder is an interesting answer to that question."

"You're one to talk," he retorted, and she sucked in a breath, her face going white, then flushing deep red.

He hated himself for that, but that was nothing new, so he kept going—as if he could explain himself to her. As if she might understand him, somehow. How sad was that? How delusional? But he couldn't seem to stop.

"The docklands project that the wedding was supposed to secure would have done what years of struggle on my part couldn't—assure the Corretti family's legacy into the future, legitimately. Bring all the warring factions of the family together." He searched her face. "How could I refuse to do something so important? Why would I? I was prepared to do my duty to my family, and I can't say I wouldn't do it again."

But she was shaking her head, and she even let out another laugh that seemed to pierce him through the chest, leaving only an icy chill in its wake.

"I've heard all of this before," she said, shrugging. "The struggle to be a good man, the weight of the family name, the call to duty. It's like a song and I know all the words." Her gaze slammed into his, and he was amazed to find it felt as if she'd used a fist instead. "But when Niccolo said it, I believed him."

CHAPTER SEVEN

NICCOLO FALCO. AGAIN. Always.

"Your beloved Niccolo is a liar and a crook," Alessandro said through his teeth. "He wouldn't know the right thing to do if it attacked him on the streets of Naples, and he certainly wouldn't do it. Don't kid yourself."

She got to her feet then, stiff and jerky, as if she thought she might break apart where she stood. "I would never lower myself to a Corretti scum like you," she'd hissed at him on that dance floor, and he'd believed her then.

He didn't know why he wanted so badly not to believe her now.

"Is this what you meant by *real,* Alessandro?" she asked in a harsh whisper, her bright eyes ablaze. "Are you satisfied?"

"It would be so much easier to simply give in," he threw at her, his voice unsteady. As if he'd lost control of himself, which was unacceptable, but he couldn't stop. "To simply be the man everyone thinks I am, anyway, no matter what I do. Even you, who shouldn't dare to throw a single stone my way for fear of what I could throw back at you. *Even you.*"

She sucked in a breath, as if he really had thrown something at her.

"Because there could be no one lower in all of Italy."

Something in the way she said it ripped at him, or maybe that was the way she looked at him, as if he'd finally managed to crush her—and he detested himself anew. "Not one person lower than me. Yet you can't keep your hands off me, can you?"

"You know exactly what kind of man Niccolo is," he said then, because he couldn't handle what her voice did to him. What that look in her eyes made him feel. "You're here at his bidding, to do whatever dirty work he requires. And it's certainly been dirty, hasn't it? But you sneer at *my* name?"

"I am here," she threw back at him, her voice still so ragged and her eyes so dark, too dark, "until we discover whether or not our recklessness results in a pregnancy neither one of us wants. We risked bringing a brand-new life into all of this bitterness and hate. That's the kind of people we are, Alessandro."

"Why don't you teach me," he said then, his gaze on hers, hot and hurt and too many other things he couldn't define and wasn't sure he wanted to know, though he could feel them all battering at him.

"Teach you what? Manners? I think we're past that."

"You're the expert on *men like me,*" he said, fascinated despite himself when she blanched at the way he said that. "You know all about it, apparently. Teach me what that means. Show me. Help me be as bad as you think I am already."

Something shifted in the air between them. In her gaze. The way her blue eyes shone with unshed misery, and the way she suddenly looked so small then, so vulnerable. So shattered.

And all he felt was…raw. Raw and ruined, all the way through to his bones.

Or maybe that was the way she looked at him.

"Let me guess what makes me the perfect teacher," she said, her voice cracking.

"You tell me, Elena," he said, his own voice a low, dark growl. "You're the one in bed with the enemy."

And she swayed then, as if he'd punched her hard in the gut. He felt as if he had, a kind of hot, bitter shame pouring over him, almost drowning him. But she steadied herself, and one hand crept over her heart, as if, he realized dimly, it ached. As if it ached straight up through her ribs, enough for her to press against it from above.

"I can't do this anymore."

Her voice was thick and unsteady, and he had the impression she didn't see him at all, though she stared right at him. Her eyes were wide and slicked with pain, and he watched in a kind of helpless horror as they finally overflowed.

"I don't..." She shook, and she wept, and it tore him apart. And then her uneven whisper smashed all the pieces. "I don't know what I'm doing here."

Alessandro reached for her then because he didn't know what else to do. Elena threw her free hand out to stop him, to warn him. Maybe even to hit him, he thought—and he'd deserve it if she did. He did yet another thing he couldn't understand, reaching out and lacing his fingers through hers, the way he had on that dance floor long ago. She shuddered, then drew in a harsh breath.

But she didn't pull away, and something in him, hard and desperate, eased.

"I can't breathe anymore," she whispered, those tears tracking down her soft cheeks. He felt the tremor in her hand, saw it shiver over her skin. "I can't breathe—"

He pulled her to him, cradling her against his chest as if she was made of glass, the need to hold her roaring in him, loud and imperative and impossible to ignore. She bowed her head into him and he felt the hand she'd held against her own heart ball into a fist against the wall of his chest.

He ran his free hand down the length of her spine and then back up. Again and again. He found himself murmuring words he didn't entirely comprehend, half-remembered words from the long-ago nannies who had soothed his nightmares and bandaged his scrapes as a boy. He bent his head down close to hers and rested his cheek on top of her head.

She shook against him, silent sobs rolling hard through her slender body, and he held her. He didn't think about how little sense this made. He didn't think about what this told him about himself, or how terrified he should be of this woman and the things she made him feel. And do. He simply held her.

And when she stopped crying and stirred against him, it was much, much harder than it should have been to let her pull away. She stepped out of his arms and dropped his hand, then scrubbed her palms over her face. And then she looked up at him, tearstained and wary with a certain resolve in her brilliant blue eyes, and something flipped over in his chest.

"I'm not a whore," she said, something naked and urgent moving over her face and through her remarkable eyes as they met his. "I'm not engaged to Niccolo. I ran out on him six months ago after he hit me, and I've been hiding from him ever since."

He only stared at her. The world, this island, his house, even he seemed to explode, devastating and silent, leaving nothing but Elena and the way she looked at him, the faint dampness against his chest where she'd sobbed against him and what she'd said. What it meant.

She was not engaged. She was not a whore. She wasn't a spy.

It beat in him, louder and louder, drowning out his own heartbeat.

"I'm risking everything I care about to tell you this," she continued, and he heard the catch in her voice, the tightness. *The fear,* he thought. *She's afraid. Of me.* "The only things I have left. So please…" She choked back a sob and it made him ache. It made him loathe himself anew. "Please, Alessandro. Prove you're who you say you are."

"A Corretti?" He hardly recognized his own voice, scratchy and rough, pulled from somewhere so deep in him he hadn't known he meant to speak.

She crossed her arms, more to hold herself than to hold him off, he thought. She took a deep breath. Then her chin lifted and her blue eyes were brave and somber as they held his, and he felt everything inside of him shift. Then roll.

"Be the man who does the right thing," she said, her voice quiet. And still it rang in him, through him, like a bell. Like a benediction he couldn't possibly deserve. "Who does his duty and would again. If that's who you are, please. Be you."

"Come," Alessandro said in a hushed voice Elena had never heard before.

She was so dazed, so hollowed out by what had happened, what she'd done, that she simply followed where he led. He ushered her out onto a small nook of a terrace that jutted out over the water, settling her into the wide, swinging chair that hung there, swaying slightly in the soft breeze.

"Wait here," he told her, and then walked away.

She couldn't have moved if she'd wanted to, she realized. She drew her knees up onto the bright white seat and leaned back. The chair swung, gently. Rocking her. Soothing her the way his hand had, warm and reassuring along her back as she'd cried. Down below, the rocky cliff fell steeply into the jagged rocks, and the sea sparkled and danced in the afternoon sun, as if everything was perfectly fine. As if none of this mattered, not really.

But Elena knew better.

She'd betrayed her family and her village and every last thing she'd clung to across all of these months, and yet somehow she couldn't seem to do anything but breathe in the crisp air, the scent of sweet flowers and cut grass in the breeze.

Almost as if she really believed she was safe. Almost as if she thought *he* was, the way she always had. When she suspected the truth was that she was simply broken beyond repair.

Alessandro returned with a damp cloth in his hand and when he squatted down before her his hard face was so serious that it made her chest feel tight. She leaned forward and let him wash the tears from her face. He was extraordinarily gentle, and it swelled in her like pain.

He pulled the cloth away and didn't move for a moment. He only looked up at her, searching her face. She had no idea what he saw.

"Tell me," he said.

It was an order as much as it was a request, and she knew she shouldn't. Her mind raced, turning over possibilities like *tavola reale* game pieces, looking for some way out of this, some way to fix what she'd done, what she'd said, what she'd confessed....

But it was too late for that.

This was the price of her foolishness, her selfishness. First Niccolo had tricked her, and then this man had hurt her feelings, and she was too weak to withstand either. Now that her tears were dry, now that she could breathe, she could see it all with perfect, horrifying clarity. She hadn't kept her village or her family's legacy safe the first time, and given the opportunity to fix that, she'd failed.

Because he thought too little of her, and she couldn't stand it.

She was more than broken, she thought then. She was a disgrace.

"Tell me what happened to you," he said then, carefully, again so very gentle that her throat constricted. "Tell me what he did."

He rose and then settled himself on the other end of the swinging chair, one leg drawn up and the other anchoring them to the floor. His hard mouth was in a firm line as he gazed at her, his dark green eyes grave. For a moment she was thrown back to that ballroom in Rome, when she'd looked up to see a stranger looking at her, exactly like this. As if the whole world hinged on what might happen next.

Which she supposed it had then. Why not again?

"I'm from a long line of very simple fishermen," she said, pushing past the lump in her throat, concentrating on her hands instead of him. "But my great-grandfather eloped with the daughter of a rich man from Fondi. Her parents begged her to reconsider, but she refused, and they decided it was better their daughter live as a rich fisherman's wife than a poor one's. They gave my great-grandfather her dowry. It was substantial."

She pulled up her knees, then wrapped her arms around her legs, fully aware that this was as close to the fetal position as she could get while sitting up. And she fought off her sense of disloyalty, the fact that she should be protecting this legacy, not handing it over to man who was perfectly capable of destroying it. On a whim.

But she didn't know what else to do.

"He was a proud man and he didn't want their money," she continued, swallowing back the self-recrimination.

"But my great-grandmother convinced him to put it toward a big stretch of land along the coast, so her family need not be as dependent on the whims of the sea as the rest of the village. And the land has been handed down ever since, from eldest son to eldest son."

She looked past him then, out toward the water, as if she could squint hard and see all the way across the waves to the remote little village she was from, tucked up in its rocky hills so far away. She could imagine every rock, every blade of grass, every tree, as if she was standing there now. She knew every house that clung to the hillside, every boat in the harbor. And most of the faces, too.

"It must," Alessandro said quietly, "be worth a great deal more now than it was then."

Elena should have thanked him, she thought, her eyes snapping back to his, for reminding her where she was. And who he was. She wasn't sharing this story with him—she was gambling everything on the slim possibility he was a better man than she thought he was. She nodded.

"It is," she said. "And my parents had only me."

"So the land is yours?" he asked, his brows lifting.

"My father is a traditional man," Elena said, looking down the sweep of her legs, staring at her feet against the bright white cushions. Anywhere but at Alessandro. "When he dies, if I'm not married, the land will be held in trust. Once I marry it will transfer to my husband. If I'm already married when he dies, my husband will get the land on our wedding day."

"Ah," Alessandro said, a cynical twist to his lips when she looked at him again. "You must have been Niccolo's dream come true."

"Last summer my father was diagnosed with a brain tumor," she told him, pushing forward because she couldn't stop now. "There was no possible way to operate." So matter-of-fact, so clinical. When it had cast her whole world into shadow. It still did. "The doctors said he had a year to live, if he was lucky."

"A year?" His dark green gaze felt like a touch. The long arm he'd stretched out along the back of the seat moved slightly, as if he meant to reach for her but thought better of it. That shouldn't have warmed her. "It's nearly July."

She hugged herself tighter, guilt and shame and that terrible grief flattening her, making it hard to breathe.

"About a month after we got the news, I was walking home one evening when a handsome stranger approached me, right there in the street," she said softly.

Alessandro's lips thinned, and he muttered something guttural and fierce in Sicilian. He looked furious again, dark and powerful, like some kind of vengeful god only pretending to sit there so civilly. Only waiting.

"Do you want to hear this?" she asked then, lifting a hand to rub at the pressure behind her temple and only then realizing that she was shaking. "All of it?"

"I told you," he said, a kind of ferocity in his voice, all that ruthlessness and demand gleaming in his dark green eyes. He touched her then, reaching over to tuck a wayward strand of her hair behind her ear, that hard mouth curving when goose bumps rose along her neck, her shoulder. "I want everything."

And Elena understood then that she was open and vulnerable to this man in ways she'd never been before. This really was everything. This was all she had left inside of her, all she'd had left to hold, laid out before him because she'd finally given in. She'd finally let go. This was everything lost, her whole world ruined, and nothing left to hope for but the possibility of his mercy.

This was surrender. Everything else had been games.

"I didn't think I was particularly naive," she said then,

because he was looking at her in that too-incisive way of his, and she was afraid of what he might see. And of what he might do when she was finished. "I'd been to university. I have a law degree. I was starting to take on all the duties and responsibilities of the family business. The land. The money. The constant development proposals." She shook her head, scowling at her own memories. Her own stupidity. "I wasn't just some silly village girl."

And that was the crux of it. She felt new tears prick at the backs of her eyes, and hurriedly blinked them back. She'd thought she was better than where she came from. She'd thought very highly of herself indeed. She'd been certain she *deserved* the handsome, wealthy stranger who had appeared like magic to sweep her off her feet.

Such vanity.

She only realized she'd said it out loud when Alessandro said something else in his brash Sicilian, so little of which she understood even after her time there. He shifted in his seat, making it swing with him as he did.

"I told you before," he said. "It was a con."

"I believed him," Elena said simply, shame and regret in her voice, moving in her veins like sludge. She felt it all over her face, and had to stop looking at him before she saw it on his, too. "I believed every single thing he told me. All of his big dreams. All of his plans. That he and I were a team." Her voice cracked, but she kept going. "That he loved me. I believed every word."

"Elena," he said in a voice she'd never heard him use before. She had to close her eyes briefly against it. As if her name was an endearment she couldn't believe a man so hard even knew. "You were supposed to believe him. He set you up."

She didn't know why she wanted to weep then, again.

"I knew you were lying to me in Rome," she said

fiercely, hugging her knees tight, keeping her eyes trained on the sea, determined to hold the tears back. "About everything. You had to be lying, because Niccolo couldn't possibly be the man you described, and because, of course, you were a Corretti."

"Of course." His tone made her wince. She didn't dare look at his expression.

"I went looking for things to prove you were a liar. One night while Niccolo slept, I got up and decided to search the laptop he took everywhere with him."

She heard Alessandro's release of breath, short and sharp, but she still couldn't look at him. Especially not now.

"He caught me, of course, but not until after I read far too many emails that explained in detail his plans for my family's land." She frowned, as horrified now as she had been then. "He wanted to build a luxury hotel, which would transform my forgotten village into a major tourist destination. We're fishermen, first and foremost. We don't even have a decent beach. We like to visit Amalfi, but we don't want to compete with it."

She shook her head, remembering that night in such stark detail. She'd only thrown on a shirt of Niccolo's and a pair of socks, and had snuck down to the kitchen to snoop on his computer while he snored. It had been cold in his villa, and she remembered shivering as she sat on one of the stools, her legs growing chillier the longer she sat there.

And she remembered the way her stomach had lurched when she'd looked up to see him in the doorway.

He hadn't asked her what she was doing. He'd only stared at her, his black eyes flat and mean, and for a terrifying moment Elena hadn't recognized him.

She'd told herself she was only being fanciful. It had been well after midnight and she hadn't heard him approach. But he was still her Niccolo, she'd assured herself.

He was in love with her, he was going to marry her, and while they were probably going to fight about his privacy and all these emails she couldn't understand, it would all be fine.

She'd been so sure.

"I asked him what it meant, because I was certain there had to be a reasonable explanation." She let out a hollow laugh. "He knew we wanted to conserve the land, protect the village. He'd spent hours talking to my father about it. He'd promised."

"I imagine he did not have a satisfying explanation," Alessandro said darkly.

"He slapped me." Such a funny, improbable word to describe it. The shock of the impact first, then the burst of pain. Then she'd hit the cold stone floor, and that had hurt even more.

Alessandro went frighteningly still.

Elena's heart raced, and she felt sick. Her knuckles were white where she gripped her own legs, and she still wanted to curl up further, disappear. But it didn't matter if he believed her, she told herself staunchly. Her own parents hadn't believed her. It only mattered that she told this truth, no matter what he thought of it.

"He slapped me so hard he knocked me down. Off my stool. To the floor." She made herself look at Alessandro then, burning there in his quiet fury, his dark green eyes brilliant with rage.

Directed at Niccolo, she understood. Not at her. And maybe that was why she told him something she'd never told anyone else. Something she'd never said out loud before.

"He called me a whore," she told him quietly. "Your whore, in fact."

Alessandro swore, and his hand twitched along the back

of the swing as if he wanted to reach through her memories, through her story, and respond to Niccolo in kind.

"When was this?" he asked, his voice hoarse.

"A few days after the ball," she said. "After..."

"Yes," he said in a low voice with too many deep currents. "After."

She let go of her iron grip on her legs before her hands went numb, and used them, shaky and cold, to scrape her hair back from her face.

"He said it was bad enough he had to marry me to get the land, but now he had to do it after I'd made him a laughingstock with his sworn enemy?" She didn't see the sea in front of her then. She only saw Niccolo's face, twisted in a rage. She saw the way he'd stood over her, so cruel, so cold, while she lay there too stunned to cry. "He told me that if I knew what was good for me, I'd shut my mouth and be thankful the land was worth more than I was. And then he walked out of the villa and left me there on the floor."

"Elena."

But she had to finish. She had to get it out or she never would, and she didn't want to think about why it was suddenly so important to her that the man she'd never thought she'd see again know every last detail. Every last way she'd made such a fool of herself.

"I left, of course," she said, ignoring the wobble in her voice and the constriction in her throat. And all of his heat and power beside her. "But I didn't really mean it. I thought there was some kind of misunderstanding. He couldn't have meant to hit me, to say those things to me. Maybe he'd been drinking. I went home to my parents, as I always did." She swallowed, hard. "And they hugged me, and told me that they loved me, and then they told me they blamed themselves that I'd turned out so spoiled, so high-strung. So selfish."

She shook her head when he started to speak and he stilled, frowning.

"They were so *kind*. Niccolo was going to be my husband, they told me, and marriages took work. Commitment. I was going to have to grow up and stop telling terrible stories when I didn't get my way." She laughed again, and it sounded broken to her own ears. "Niccolo was a good man, they said, and I believed them. I *wanted* to believe them. It was easier to believe that I'd made up the whole thing than that he was the person I'd seen that night."

Alessandro shifted, and put his arm around her, then gathered her close to his side. Holding her again. Holding her close, as if he could fight off all her demons that easily. She wondered if he could, if he even wanted to bother, and her eyes slicked over with a glaze of heat.

"He laughed when I rang him," she whispered. "He told me that I was a stupid bitch. A whore. He told me I had twenty-four hours to get back to the villa and if I didn't he'd come get me himself, and I would really, truly regret it. That he didn't care if he had to marry me in a wheelchair."

Alessandro's arm tightened around her, and she allowed herself the comfort of his heat, his strength, even though she knew it was fleeting at best. That it wasn't hers, no matter how much it felt as if it was. That he was far more dangerous to her now, armed with all of the knowledge she'd given him, even if he really was the man he claimed he was.

Neither one of them spoke for a long while. His hand moved over her hair, stroking her as if she was something precious to him. She accepted that she wished she was. That she always had. That she'd wanted too much from him from the start, and had been paying for it ever since.

"And that time," she said when she could speak again, giving him everything he'd asked for, everything she'd been hiding, *everything*, "I believed him."

* * *

Alessandro stood on the balcony outside his bedroom long after midnight, staring out into the dark.

He couldn't sleep. He could hardly think straight. Once again, she'd shoved his world off its axis, and he was still reeling.

"Why didn't you tell me sooner?" he'd asked her as the light began to change, still holding her on the swinging chair, pulling her closer as the wind picked up.

"You would never have believed me."

"Perhaps," he'd said, but she'd only smiled. "Perhaps, in time, I might have."

But she'd been right. He would have thought it was another game. He would have laughed at her. Hated her all the more. He would have treated her exactly the same—worse, even. He couldn't pretend otherwise.

He balled his hands into fists against the rail now, scowling.

He should have known. He had been too busy concentrating on the darkness in him, too busy nursing his wounded pride. The truth had always been there, staring him in the face. In every kiss, every touch. In the way she'd given herself to him so unreservedly.

In what he'd known about her the moment he'd seen her in Rome.

He should have tried to reach her then. Instead, he'd stormed off that dance floor and left her to be brutalized. He'd put her through hell all on his own. And he couldn't blame his family for that. That had been all him.

He was no different from them at all. He couldn't imagine how he'd ever believed otherwise.

He sensed her behind him a moment before she stepped to the rail beside him, hugging herself against the cool night air.

"I didn't mean to wake you," he said.

She smiled, but she didn't look at him. "You didn't."

He watched her, feeling something work through him, something powerful and new and all about that tilt to her jaw, that perfect curve of her hip, the way she squared her shoulders as she stood there. Her lovely strength. Her courage.

He didn't have the slightest idea what to do with any of it. Or with her.

Alessandro couldn't help but touch her then, his hands curving over her bare shoulders and turning her to face him. She was as beautiful in the shadows as she was in the light, though the wariness in her gaze made his chest ache. He wanted to protect her, to keep her safe. From Niccolo. From the world.

Even from himself.

He stroked his fingers down her lovely face, and felt the way she shivered, heard the way she sighed. He thought of that first touch, so long ago now, that glorious heat. He thought of that marvelous glow between them. That easy, instant perfection.

And all of it was true.

Everything he'd felt. Everything he'd imagined. Everything he'd wanted then, and thought impossible.

"What happens now?" she asked softly, her eyes searching his.

He smiled then, over the rawness inside of him, the dangerous, insidious hope.

"Now?" he asked, his voice gruff. As uneven as he felt. "I apologize."

And then he kissed her, gently, and she melted into him. Like the first time all over again. Better.

Real.

Elena woke in his wide bed, safe and warm.

She lay on her side and gazed out at the morning light,

the blue sky, and the previous afternoon came back to her slowly, drip by drip. Then the night. The way he'd picked her up so gently and carried her back to bed. The way he'd moved over her, worshipping every part of her, taking his time and driving her into a sweet, wild oblivion, before curling around her and holding her close as they fell asleep together.

It had been so different, Elena thought now. She smiled to herself. It had felt like—

But she pushed that thought away, afraid to look at it too closely. Her stomach began to ache, and she cursed herself. Things were precarious enough already. There were any number of ways Alessandro could use what she'd told him against her. No need to tangle her emotions any further. No need to make it that much worse.

No need to walk straight into another disaster as blindly as she had the first.

She climbed from the bed and started for the bathroom, aware with each step that she didn't feel well—as if her body was finally taking all of the past weeks' excesses out on her. As if it was punishing her. She had a slight headache. Her stomach hurt. Even her breasts ached. And she felt heavy, all the way through. Almost as if—

She stopped in her tracks and, for a moment, was nothing at all but numb. Then she walked into the bathroom, confirmed her suspicion and had only just come back out again and pulled on the first thing she could find—the long-sleeved shirt he'd been wearing the night before, as it happened—when Alessandro walked through the bedroom door.

He had his mobile phone clamped to his ear, a fierce scowl on his beautiful face, and Elena simply stood there, helplessly, and stared. Everything had changed. Again.

She didn't have any idea how this would go, or what might happen next.

And he still made her heart beat faster when he walked into a room. He still made her knees feel weak. All this time, and she hadn't grown used to him at all. All of these weeks, and if anything, she was even more susceptible to him than she had been at the start.

She didn't dare think about what that meant, either. She was terribly afraid she already knew.

"I don't care," he growled into the phone. He raked an impatient hand through his hair. "I'm running out of ways to tell you that, Mother, and I ran out of patience ten minutes ago. None of this has anything to do with me."

He hung up, then tossed the phone on the bed. His dark green eyes narrowed when they found hers. He stilled, that restlessness she could see written all over him fading.

"Has something happened?" Elena asked, and she could hear the nerves in her voice. The panic. His gaze sharpened, telling her he did, too.

"Just one more scandal linked to the Corretti name, though this time, happily, not mine," he said. "Or not entirely mine, though it gives rise to all sorts of speculation I should probably care about." His focus was on Elena, his dark green eyes speculative as they swept over her face. "Alessia Battaglia is pregnant."

Elena swallowed. "Oh," she said.

She wished she wasn't wearing only his shirt. It was like déjà vu. The last time she'd worn a man's shirt— But she couldn't let herself think that way. It would only make this harder.

"Well," she said lamely. She had to clear her throat. "I...am not."

For a long moment, there was only the sound of her heartbeat, loud in her ears. And the way he looked at her across the expanse of his bed, that fierce and arrogant face of his unreadable.

"You're sure?" he asked.

Her throat was dry. "I am."

She didn't know what she expected. But it wasn't the way his face changed, the way his eyes darkened—a brief, searing flash. It wasn't the way that pierced her, straight to the bone.

Regret.

That was what she saw on his face, in his dark gaze. For a dizzying moment, she couldn't breathe.

Because she felt it, too, like a newer, deeper ache. As if they'd lost something today. As if they should grieve this instead of celebrate it, and that didn't make any kind of sense at all.

"All right," he said then. "That's good news, isn't it?"

She nodded, because she didn't trust her voice.

"We must be lucky," he said quietly. But his smile was like a ghost, and it hurt her.

It all hurt.

And she knew why, she thought then, in dawning understanding and a surge of fear. This hadn't been about the games they played, or any of the things she'd been telling herself so fiercely for so long. The lust and the hurt and the wild, uncontrollable passion had been no more than window dressing, and she'd been desperately ignoring what lay beyond all of that since the moment she'd laid eyes on this man in Rome.

Because it shouldn't have happened like that. It shouldn't have happened at all. Love at first sight was nonsense; it belonged in poems, songs. Sentimental films. Real people made choices, they didn't take one look at a stranger on a dance floor and feel the world shift around them, a key turning in a lock.

Elena had been telling herself that for months, and here she was anyway, not carrying his child and as absurdly upset about it as if they'd been trying to get pregnant instead of simply unpardonably reckless.

She was in love with him, God help her. *She was in love with him.*

It rang in her, long and low and deep. And it wasn't new. It had been there from that very first glance. It had happened that fast, that irrevocably, and she simply hadn't wanted to accept that it could be true. But it was.

And now she simply had to figure out how to survive the end of her time with him, the end of these months that had changed her life forever, without giving him that last, worst weapon to use against her.

"Yes," she agreed, aware he was watching her with those clever eyes of his and she knew he saw too much, the way he always did. "Very lucky."

CHAPTER EIGHT

THE FORTIETH DAY dawned with no less than three emails from his assistant detailing the precise time the helicopter would arrive to transport him back to Sicily, and Alessandro still wasn't ready.

He'd run out of excuses. He had to return home or risk damaging Corretti Media in a way he might not be able to fix, and despite his attempts to cut off the part of him that cared about that, he knew he couldn't let it happen. He was the CEO, and he was needed. And he had to deal with his family before they all imploded, something his mother's daily, increasingly hysterical voice-mail messages suggested was imminent.

He had to go back to his life. His attempt to leave it behind had only ever been a temporary measure, a reaction to that cursed wedding. It wasn't him. Duty, responsibility—they beat in him still, and grew louder by the day.

But he couldn't leave Elena. Not now that he'd discovered she was the woman he'd believed she was from the start. Not now that everything had changed.

He didn't know what she wanted, however, and the uncertainty was like a fist in his gut. It had been hard enough to convince her to remain on the island once she'd discovered she wasn't pregnant.

"There's no reason to stay here any longer." She'd at-

tempted that calm, cool smile he hated and he'd taken pleasure in the fact she couldn't quite pull it off, sitting there
so primly in the sitting area of his bedchamber, dressed
only in one of his shirts and all of the smooth, bare flesh
of her legs on display. "Our arrangement was based entirely around waiting to find out—"

"That arrangement was based on the premise that you
were still engaged to Niccolo Falco," he'd said, cutting her
off. "Working for him, in fact. A spy." He'd smiled. "You
are none of those things, *cara.*"

"Most importantly, I'm not pregnant," she'd argued,
with a stubborn tilt to her chin. "What you thought about
me until yesterday is irrelevant, really."

"Do you think he's still searching for you?" he'd asked
calmly when he'd wanted nothing more than to put his
mouth on her—to remind her how they were anything but
irrelevant. And despite that black punch of murderous rage
that slammed into him at the thought of Niccolo.

"I know he is," she'd said with a shrug. "He sends me
an email every week or so, to make sure I never forget it."
She'd smiled then, but it was far too bitter. "It was a good
thing I stopped waitressing and took the yacht job. He was
in Cefalù only a few days behind me."

He'd had to force his violent fury down, shove it under
wraps, before he'd been able to say another word—and
even then, the dark pulse of his temper was in every clipped
syllable.

"Do you really believe I will simply let you go like
this?" he'd asked. "Wash my hands of you and go about
my business while that bastard runs you into the ground?
What makes you think that's a possibility?"

Something he hadn't been able to identify chased over
her face then, but had echoed in him all the same.

"It's not your decision," she'd said after a moment. "It's mine."

They'd stared at each other for a long while.

"You must know I can keep you here," he'd said quietly. "No one comes or goes from this place without my permission."

"You won't do something like that," she'd replied with conviction, her eyes meeting his. Holding. "You're better than that."

And, damn her, he'd wanted to be.

He'd reached over to take her hands in his, threading his fingers through hers, then pulling their joined hands up to his mouth. She'd sighed, her eyes filling with all of that heat and passion that had delivered them here in the first place. And he'd willed her to relent. To bend. To yield.

To want to hold on to him the way he needed to hold on to her.

"You're the one who wanted forty days," he'd said, searching her face, trying to see what he needed to see written there. "There's almost a whole week left."

She'd shaken her head. "Playtime is over, Alessandro."

"Forty days," he'd repeated, because he hadn't known what else to say, how else to convince her. She couldn't leave. This wasn't over—it had only just begun.

"Alessandro…"

"Elena. Please." He hadn't recognized his own voice, much less what coursed through him as he'd said it. "Stay."

He'd begged. There was no other word for it.

But she'd looked up at him then and he hadn't cared at all that he'd bent in a way he'd previously believed impossible. He'd only cared that it worked.

"I'll give you forty days," she'd said when he'd begun to lose hope, her eyes changing from blue to gray. "But that's it. This can't go on any longer than that."

He'd only moved closer to her, and then he'd taken her mouth with his, answering her as best he could.

It had all gone by too quickly, he thought now, glaring out his window at the sea as if it had betrayed him. As if nature and time had conspired against him. He sensed her come into the master suite before he heard her, that familiar spark of lightning down his spine and straight into his sex—and that fist in his gut seemed to burrow deeper.

"Are you ready?" he asked without turning around. He had to fight to keep his voice level, to keep his temper under control, and it was much harder than it should have been. How could he lose her when he'd just found her? "The helicopter will be here any moment."

"Of course," Elena said, back to that smooth voice he loathed. "I packed everything that's mine."

"And my staff packed everything else," he said evenly. "What use do you imagine I have for the clothes you wore while you were here?"

She didn't answer. He shoved his hands into his pockets so she wouldn't see that he'd balled them into fists. He knew she was still standing there—he could feel her—but the silence stretched out between them, sharp and treacherous. He didn't know what to do, or say.

He only knew he couldn't stand this.

Alessandro heard the unmistakable sound of his helicopter then, roaring toward the meadow for its landing. Coming down fast to hasten this unacceptable ending.

Too late, he thought. *It's always too late.*

He turned then, abruptly, and caught the look on her face. Resolute. Miserable. Brave and determined. He concentrated on *miserable*.

"Stay with me," he bit out. An order this time, with no silk or seduction or even begging to sweeten it.

"Stay?" she echoed, as if she didn't understand the word.

"Here?" She shook her head, sketched that airy smile. "You can't keep hiding away here, Alessandro. It's time to go home."

She was dressed for the outside world. No flowing dress, no tiny shorts, no skimpy bikini. She wore those white denim trousers that made him uncomfortably hard, another pair of wicked heels and a peach-colored top that flirted with her curves beneath a cream-colored scarf looped lazily around her neck. Her hair was slicked back into a sleek ponytail, and she had sunglasses perched on her head, ready to slide over her eyes. She looked casually fashionable, impenetrably lovely, and he knew it was armor.

He hated it.

"Come to Palermo with me," he threw out without thinking, but it didn't matter. He didn't care how complicated that could become. He didn't care if it started a damned war with the Falco family. He'd fight it with his own bare hands if he had to. He didn't care about anything but her.

And if an alarm sounded deep inside of him then, he ignored it.

"You know that's impossible," she said fiercely. As if he'd finally struck a nerve. "You know I have to go."

Alessandro remembered that night, so long ago now, when he'd told her he would chase her through the house if she wanted him to do it. That he would let her abdicate any responsibility for what happened between them, let it all be on him, if that was what it took. Was that what she needed?

But he couldn't do it.

"I won't hold you against your will. I won't even beg." His voice was low, but all of their history was in it. That dance. This island. All the truths they'd finally laid bare. "Come with me anyway."

"This isn't fair," she whispered, and he shouldn't have

taken it as a kind of harsh victory that she sounded as ago-
nized as he felt. As torn apart. "We agreed."

"Just this once," he said fiercely, "just this one time,
admit what's happening here. What's always been happening here. For God's sake, Elena—come with me because
you can't bear to leave me."

Whole worlds moved through her gaze then, and left
the overbright sheen of tears in their wake. And it wasn't
enough, that he knew she wanted him, too, that he knew
exactly how stark her need was. That he could feel it inside of him, lighting up his own. That he knew he could
exploit it, with a single touch.

He needed her to admit it. To say it. He needed all of this
to matter to her. And the fact that he was uncomfortable
with the intensity of that need—that it edged into territory
he refused to explore—didn't make it any less necessary.

A moment dragged by, too sharp and too hard. Then
another.

"I'm not a good person," she said finally. Her hands
opened and closed fitfully, restlessly, at her sides. "And
neither are you. A good person would never have allowed
what happened between us in Rome to happen at all. I was
engaged. And you knew I was with Niccolo when you approached me." Her gaze slammed into his. "All we do is
make mistakes, Alessandro. Maybe that's all this is. Maybe
that's what we should admit."

He started toward her, watching her face as he drew
closer. He had never been so uncertain of anything or anyone in his life, and yet so oddly sure of her at the same
time. So sure of *this*. He didn't understand it. But like everything with Elena, from that very first glance, it simply
was. Undefinable. Undeniable. But always and ever *his*.

"I know that you don't trust me," he said when he
reached her, looking down into her troubled blue gaze. "I

know what the name Corretti means to you. I know you think all manner of terrible things about me, and I know you're waiting for the next blow." He reached over to trace the vulnerable curve of her mouth with his thumb, making her tremble. "Come to Palermo. Have faith."

He read the storms in her eyes, across her pretty face. And he forced himself to do nothing at all but wait it out. Wait her out.

"I don't believe in faith anymore." A great cloud washed over her, across her face and through those beautiful eyes, and left them shadowed. She pulled in a deep, long breath, then let it out. "But I'll do it," she said finally, as if the words were wrenched from her. "I'll come with you."

Satisfaction and intense relief ripped through him, making him feel bigger. Wilder. Edgy with a ferocious kind of triumph.

But he wasn't finished.

"Tell me why."

Her eyes darkened, and she started to shake her head, started to retreat from him. He slid his hand along her jaw, and held her like that, forcing her to look at him. Keeping her right there in plain sight. Her lips parted slightly, and her breath came hard, as if she was running away the way she no doubt wished she was.

"Tell me," he said quietly. "I need to hear you say it."

She gazed back at him. He could feel her pulse against his hand, could see it wild and panicked in her throat. "Because…" she began, and had to stop, as if her throat closed in on her. Her eyes were filled with heat and damp. She swayed on her feet as if there was a great wind howling around them, and it threatened to knock her flat.

But she didn't fall.

He brushed the knuckles of his other hand over her soft cheek, her distractingly elegant cheekbone.

"Say it," he whispered.

"Because I can't leave you," she said finally, in a broken, electrifying rush. He felt it from the top of his head to the bottom of his feet, as if he'd been struck by lightning, by her, all over again. As if she'd shone that bright light into all of that darkness within him, chasing it away at last. "Not yet."

The helicopter ride was bumpy and noisy, despite the bulky headphones she'd been given to wear, but Elena was happy enough to stay silent while Alessandro and the assistant who'd flown out to meet him discussed Corretti Media business concerns. She soaked in the beckoning Mediterranean blue far below, and pretended the only thing in her head was the sea. The golden sun. The lovely view.

But it didn't work. The enormity of what she'd done was like iron in her chest, making it harder and harder to breathe. It had been one thing to hand over her body, another still to offer up her story to his mercy, such as it was. But she was very much afraid that, today, Alessandro had demanded she give him her soul.

And she'd done it.

She couldn't believe she'd actually done it.

Too soon, the helicopter was making its way through the Palermo skyline, and then setting down on the roof of the landmark Corretti Media tower. Elena climbed out slowly, staying behind Alessandro and the assistant who hadn't stopped talking in all this time, trying to pretend she was not in the least bit overwhelmed. That she gave away her soul like it was little more than a trinket every day of the week. That she was in control of this.

"Signorina Calderon and I are going to eat something," Alessandro said then, breaking into his assistant's stream of chatter in a steely tone she'd never heard before. It brought Elena back to the present with a jolt.

"But, sir," his assistant said in a rush. "Since you've been gone, your family…" His voice trailed off as Alessandro glared at him, but he visibly rallied. "The Battaglia situation is only getting more heated, and time is nearly up for the new docklands proposal—"

"I will come into the office later, Giovanni," Alessandro said with wintry finality.

Elena's stomach twisted. He was cold, harsh, commanding—but with none of that dark fire she knew so well beneath it. This must be Alessandro, the much-feared and much-respected CEO. Alessandro, the eldest Corretti heir. No wonder people spoke of him in such awed, cowed tones. He was terrifying.

"My apologies," his assistant said smoothly, inclining his head. "Of course, that is perfect. We will expect you after lunch."

"If you want me to sign those papers," Alessandro continued in an impatient tone, stalking across the rooftop toward the entrance to the building, "I suggest you do it in the elevator. Quietly."

Elena walked faster as Alessandro's assistant got on his mobile, ordering the car brought around and demanding that someone make sure that Alessandro's favorite table was waiting for him. She reminded herself to breathe as she stepped into the shiny, gold-plated elevator where Alessandro waited, looking for all the world like a surly, caged animal. Dangerous and unpredictable.

The elevator started its descent. Alessandro signed the papers his assistant handed him on a hardbacked folder, one after the next. Without bothering to read them, Elena thought in some surprise—but then he scowled down at one of them.

"These terms are unacceptable. As both you and Di Rossi are well aware."

"He insisted that you had caved," his assistant said mildly, as if he heard that tone from Alessandro every day.

"Send it back," Alessandro ordered. "If he has a problem with it, tell him he can take it up with me personally."

His assistant's brows rose. That was obviously a threat.

The elevator stopped smoothly, discharging Alessandro's assistant on one of the higher floors, and then the doors swished shut and they were alone again. Elena told herself there was no reason at all to be so nervous. Alessandro lounged against the far wall of the car, looking deceptively languid in what was clearly a bespoke suit, the way it marveled over every fine line of his physique. The bright golden walls seemed to shrink into her as the car kept moving. His dark green eyes found hers, and Elena's heart picked up speed.

"Second thoughts?" he asked softly. A challenge.

"You're a very formidable man," she said. "Do you enjoy it?"

He only watched her, that arrogant face a study in careless, encompassing masculine power. His dark brows rose in query.

"Wielding that kind of authority like that," she said. "Making that poor man jump through your hoops without even the faintest pretense of politeness."

Dark green eyes lit with amusement. "Are you calling me rude, Elena? Or just a bad boss?"

"If that's how you treat your employees, I shudder to think how you treat your enemies." She smiled coolly. "Oh, but wait. I already know."

Alessandro's mouth crooked. "Point taken," he said gruffly, surprising her. "I apologize."

"Your assistant is very likely weeping in the toilet,"

she continued, her tone dry, burying her confusion. Alessandro? Apologizing? "Don't feel you have to apologize to *me*."

"For the record," he said, laughter in his voice, "'that poor man' comforts himself with a new Maserati every fiscal year. He's certainly not weeping as he cashes his paycheck."

"If you say so."

"Come here." His voice dropped, became something else. Something that wound through her like honey, golden and slow, making it hard to remember that he even had an assistant, or why on earth she cared.

"You're at your place of business," she said primly, but she went to him, anyway. "Smiting down every assistant in your path, apparently. All in a day's work, no doubt."

He slid a hand around to the back of her neck and then tugged her off balance so she sprawled against his chest.

This was familiar, finally. His scent, his heat. That gleam in his eyes. Her immediate reaction, molten and hot. And only as it washed through her did she understand how much she'd needed the reminder. That it didn't matter how formidable he might seem here. How distant. That this was still theirs, this electric current. This need.

It was why she was here.

"Ah, Elena," he murmured, simply holding her there against the wall of his chest, his thumb moving against her nape, his expression so intent it made her knees feel like water. "What am I going to do with you?"

"Do you mean in general or in this elevator?" she asked, aware of the breathlessness in her voice, the pounding desire that she had no doubt he could see all over her, the way he always did.

His mouth curved. "I already know what I'm going to do to you in this elevator," he told her, his other hand wrapping around her hip and pulling her against him, letting her feel how much he wanted her. His voice lowered to that sexy growl that lit her up, heating her blood, making her melt. "It might be acrobatic, but I think you can handle it."

Elena heard the *ping* that announced they'd arrived at the ground floor, but Alessandro didn't move. Her hands were pressed against the fascinating muscles of his perfect torso as she arched into him. It wasn't enough, and she didn't care where she was. This was his company—let him care. She lifted herself up on her toes and moved her mouth so close to his that if she licked her lips, she'd taste him.

"Go ahead, then," she whispered, daring him. "Show me some acrobatics."

On some level she was vaguely aware of the elevator doors sliding open, but all that mattered was Alessandro. That dark, consuming green gaze. That familiar fire, still so devastating and far too hot. As if he blacked out everything else.

He laughed, sex and heat and delicious challenge, and she shivered in anticipation, because she knew that sound, she knew its sensual promise—

And everything exploded.

Flashing lights, shouting. The press of too many bodies, the harsh slap of all that noise—

It took her too long to make sense of it—to understand that a scrum of paparazzi crowded into the open elevator door, cameras snapping and tape rolling, while Elena was still plastered against Alessandro's chest, clinging to him, announcing their relationship in stark, unmistakable terms.

But then she understood, and that was worse.

It was the end of the world as she knew it, right there and then.

Elena couldn't stop pacing.

Alessandro's penthouse spread out over the top of the

Corretti Media tower, three stories in all. It was magnificent. Glass, steel and granite, yet decorated with a deep appreciation of color and comfort. Lush Persian carpets stretched in front of fireplaces and brightened halls. Stunning, impressive art hung on the high walls, all bold colors and graceful lines. He favored deep chairs, dark woods, and all of it somehow elegant and male. Uniquely him.

And she couldn't enjoy any part of it. She could hardly see it through her panic.

"Of course he'll see the pictures," she said, not for the first time, worrying her lower lip with her fingers as she stared out the great windows. "You can count on it."

Alessandro was sprawled on one of his couches, a tablet computer in his hand. He shot a dark, unreadable look in her direction, but he didn't answer. But then, Elena was really only talking to herself.

He'd dealt with the paparazzi as best he could. He'd stepped in front of her, concealing her from view. He'd alerted his security, then whisked her up to his penthouse and hidden her away from any more cameras.

"Jackals," he'd snarled when the elevator doors finally closed again, leaving them in peace once more. "Nothing but scavengers."

But it was too late. The damage was already done.

Elena's head had spun wildly. She'd let him lead her out of the elevator bank and into his opulent home, and as soon as he'd closed that heavy penthouse door behind them she'd grabbed hold of the nearest wall and sunk down to the floor. Six months of fear and adrenaline and grief had coalesced inside of her and then simply...broken open. Flooding her.

"Don't you understand?" she'd cried. "Niccolo will see those pictures! He'll know exactly where I am! It will take him, what? A matter of *hours* to get to Palermo?"

Alessandro had gazed down at her, an enigmatic expression on his hard face.

"He won't go through me to get at you," he'd said. "He's a coward."

"I'm thrilled for you that you don't have to take him seriously," she'd thrown at him. "But I do. Believe me, Alessandro. *I do.*"

"Elena."

She'd hated the way he said her name then, the way it coiled in her, urging her to trust he'd somehow make this go away. To *have faith.*

"You can't make this disappear simply because you command it," she'd told him, caught between weariness and despair. "You have no idea how devious he is, or how determined."

"If you must insult me," Alessandro had said then, "please spare my security detail. Aside from today's disaster, they're very good at their jobs."

"For how long?" she'd demanded. "A week or two? Another forty days? When will you tire of this—of me?" She'd stared up at him, daring him to contradict her. Daring him to argue. "Because when that day comes, as we both know it will, Niccolo will be waiting. If I have faith in anything, it's that."

Alessandro's expression had shuttered, but he'd only held her gaze for a strained moment before turning on his heel, murmuring something about unavoidable paperwork and walking out. Leaving her there on his floor to drive herself out of her head with worry and the cold, hard fear that had spurred her on all this time.

The fear she'd set aside when she'd been on Alessandro's island. When she'd been safe.

She had to leave, she thought now, frowning out the towering windows at the coming dark. She had to run while she still could. That was the obvious conclusion she'd been circling around and around, not wanting to admit it was the only thing that made sense.

Because he'd been right. She didn't want to leave him. She loved him. It was that simple and that complicated. It always had been.

She turned to look at him then. He was so impossibly, powerfully beautiful. He'd stunned her from the start. And now she knew how that proud jaw tasted. She could lose herself for hours in his hard, cynical mouth. She knew what he could do with those elegant hands of his, with every part of his lean, hard frame. She knew that he felt deeply, and darkly, and that there were mysteries in him she desperately wanted to solve. She knew he'd comforted her, soothing something in her she'd thought ripped forever raw. She knew what it was like when he laughed, when he teased her, when he told her stories. She wanted all of this to be real, for him to be the man she so desperately wanted to believe he was.

She wanted to have faith. She wanted to stay.

God, how she wanted to stay.

He'd thrown off his jacket when he'd returned to the penthouse, lost his tie and loosened the top buttons of his shirt. He looked like what he was. The infinitely dangerous, ruthless and clever CEO of Corretti Media. A man of great wealth and even greater reach. The man who'd taken her body, her painful history, her heart and even her soul. And would take much more than that, she had no doubt. If she let him. If she stayed.

But he didn't love her. She didn't kid herself that he ever would. He spoke only of *want*.

This was sex. Need. A shockingly intense connection mixed with explosive chemistry. Clear all of that away and Elena was as on her own as the day she'd realized even her parents' home wasn't safe for her, and had gone on the run. The past forty days had been nothing but consuming lust, blinding fireworks, and all of it a distraction from that ugly little truth.

He looked up then, his dark green eyes searing and too incisive.

"They've been posted," he said without inflection.

That was it, then. The paparazzi pictures were online. The clock had started ticking. She had to assume Niccolo was on his way even now. Which meant she was standing here on borrowed time.

"I have to go," she said, quick and fierce, before she could talk herself out of it. Before he could. "I have to leave immediately."

"And may I ask where you plan to go?" That cool CEO's voice. It felt like nails against her skin. "Do you have a plan or are you simply...running away? Again?"

"It doesn't matter where I go," she said, trying so hard to keep all of her feelings out of this. They could only hurt her—and so could Niccolo. It was better to think of him, and run. "So long as it's far from here."

Alessandro tossed his tablet to one side. He gazed at her for a long while, as if he'd never seen her before. As if he saw too much.

Elena repressed an involuntary shiver, and found she couldn't breathe.

"I think you should marry me," he said.

CHAPTER NINE

HER HEART STOPPED in her chest.

Elena stared at him. She couldn't move. She certainly couldn't speak.

Alessandro shrugged, as if what he'd said was as casual as an invitation to coffee, though his dark green eyes were shrewd. They didn't leave her face.

"It's the only way to beat Niccolo at his own game," he said. So matter-of-fact. So calm, so controlled. As if this was nothing but one more contract that required his signature, and not one he needed to read all that closely. "Running from him hasn't worked. How else can this end?"

"It will end when my father dies," she said, though her tongue felt as numb as the rest of her. She was dimly surprised it worked at all. "I'm the executor of the trust. Obviously, he won't be able to manipulate me the way he's manipulated my father."

"He told you he would put you in a wheelchair if necessary," Alessandro reminded her with an edge in his voice and too much dark in his eyes. "He's not going to stop. In fact, he's likely to club you over the head and marry you while you're in a coma."

Elena couldn't think. The room had started revolving around her, whirling in lopsided, drunken circles. She was afraid she might fall over. She ignored the kick of hard, fierce joy inside her, because this wasn't real. It couldn't be real. And if it was? Then it was simply one more game. It wasn't something she should be joyful about.

But it only kicked harder.

"I don't think the solution is to marry you instead," she managed to say.

"Yes, of course," he said then with definite edge that time. "Because you are opposed to marrying for practical reasons, if memory serves. Or is it that you'd prefer to be dragged to the altar by your hair, to the delightful wedding music of Niccolo's abusive threats?"

"This isn't practical" was all she could think of to say.

"He won't touch you if you're my wife," Alessandro replied, steel and fire in his gaze. "The impetus to do so would disappear the moment we said our vows. If you're married, the land is no longer in any dispute. It becomes mine, and your problem is solved."

"On our wedding day," Elena heard herself say from somewhere far away. She couldn't make sense of the words. Or anything else.

His dark eyes gleamed. Something male and primitive moved over his face, then was gone. *Hidden,* something inside of her whispered, but what could he have to hide? He shrugged again, then reached beside him for the tablet, dismissing her.

As if none of this mattered to him, either way. As if this was a minor favor he'd thought he might do her, nothing more.

"Do you really think I'll let you go like this?" he'd asked a week ago on the island, so fiercely. "Wash my hands of you?"

She'd wanted to believe that he wouldn't—that he couldn't. She still did.

"Your choice, Elena."

He wasn't even looking at her. As if this conversation, his proposal of marriage, hardly maintained his interest. But she didn't believe that, either. He was not a man who begged, and yet he had. Surely that meant something. Didn't it have to mean something?

"I know you have strong feelings about the Corretti name," he said in the same offhanded way, "but all you have to do is take it and this insanity ends. It's simple."

It wasn't simple, she thought in a wash of something like anguish. It was anything but simple.

But even as she opened her mouth to refuse him—to do the sane thing and leave him, leave Sicily, save herself the only way she knew how—Elena knew she wouldn't do it. She would take him any way she could have him, even marry him under these questionable circumstances, knowing he would never feel the way she felt.

Nothing had changed. She was the same selfish, foolish girl she'd ever been. She wanted yet another man to love her when she knew that no matter what she'd thought she glimpsed in him now and again, this was nothing more than a game to him, and she no more than another piece on a chessboard he controlled. Eventually, he would grow tired of her. He would leave her.

And yet some part of her was still vain enough to think he might change his mind, that *she* might change it. Still silly enough to risk everything on that slim, unlikely chance.

She hadn't learned a thing in all this time.

"By all means," he said then, languidly scrolling down a page on his tablet, "take your time agonizing over the only reasonable choice available to you. I'm happy to wait."

Could she do it? Could she surrender the most important thing of all—the one thing even Niccolo had never got his hands on? The entire future of her village. Her family's heritage. The land. All because she so desperately hoped that Alessandro was different. That he really would do the right thing.

Because she loved him.

Idiot. The voice in her head was scathing.

Elena jerked herself around and stared out his impressive windows at the lights of the city spread out before her, but what she saw were her parents' faces. Her poor parents. They deserved so much better than this. Than her.

"What a romantic proposal." She shut her eyes. She hated herself. But she couldn't seem to stop the inevitable. She was as incapable of saving herself now as she'd been on that dance floor. And as guilty. "How can I possibly refuse?"

Late that night, Alessandro stood in the door of his bedroom and watched Elena sleep. She was curled up in his bed, and the sight of her there made the savage creature in him want to shout out his triumph to the moon. He almost did. He felt starkly possessive. Wildly victorious.

He could wake her, he knew. She would turn to him eagerly—soft and warm from sleep, and take him inside of her without a word. She would sigh slightly, sweetly, and wrap herself around him, then bury her face in his neck as he moved in her.

She'd done it so many times before.

But tonight was different. Tonight she'd agreed to become his wife.

His wife.

He hadn't known he'd meant to offer marriage until he had. And once he had, he'd understood that there was no other acceptable outcome to this situation. No alternative. She needed to be his, without reservation or impediment.

It had to be legal. It had to last. He didn't care what trouble that might cause.

There were words for what was happening to him, Alessandro knew, but he wasn't ready to think about that. Not until he'd secured her, made her his. He turned away from the bed and forced himself to head down the stairs.

Down in his home office, he sat at his wide, imposing desk and frowned down at all of the work Giovanni had prepared for his review. But he didn't flip open the top report and start reading. He found himself staring at the photo that sat on the corner of his desk instead.

It was a family shot he'd meant to get rid of ever since his grandmother had given it to him years ago. All of the Correttis were gathered around his grandmother, Teresa, at her birthday celebration eight years ago. Canny old Salvatore was smirking at the camera, holding one of Teresa's hands in his, looking just as Alessandro remembered him—as if death would never dare take him.

Alessandro's father and uncle, alive and at war with each other, stood with their wives and children on either side of Teresa, who had long been the single unifying force in the family. Her birthday, at her insistence, was the one day of the year the Correttis came together, breathed the same air, refrained from spilling blood or hideous secrets and pretended they were a real family.

Alessandro sighed, and reached over to pick up the photograph. His uncle and four cousins looked like some kind of near mirror image of his own side of the family, faces frozen into varying degrees of mutiny and forced smiles, all stiffly acquiescing to the annual charade. They were all the same, in the end. All of them locked into this family, their seedy history, this bitter, futile fight. Sometimes he found himself envious of Angelo, the only family member missing from the picture, because at least he'd been spared the worst of it.

His sister, Rosa—because he couldn't think of her any other way, he didn't care who her father was—smiled genuinely. Alessandro and Santo stood close together, looking as if they were biting back laughter, though Alessandro could no longer remember what about. His father glared, as haughty and arrogant as he'd been to his grave. And his mother looked as she always did: ageless and angry. Always so very, very angry.

"You should never have stayed away so long," she'd seethed at him earlier today. "It looks like weakness. As if you've been off licking your wounds while your cousin has stolen your bride and made our side of the family the butt of every joke in Palermo!"

"Let him," Alessandro had retorted.

"Surely you don't plan to let the insult stand?" Carmela Corretti had gasped. "Our family's honor demands—"

"Honor?" Alessandro had interrupted her icily. "Not the word I'd choose, Mother. And certainly not if I were you."

She'd sucked in a breath, as if he'd wounded her.

But Alessandro knew the woman who'd raised him. He knew her with every hollow, bitter, blackened part of his Corretti soul. She was immune to hurt. And she always returned a slap with cannon fire.

"You're just like your father," she'd said viciously. And it had speared straight through him, hitting its mark. "All of that polish and pretense on the surface, and rotten to the core within. And we know where that leads, don't we?"

He was so tired of this, he thought now. Of this feud that rolled on and on and did nothing but tear them all apart. Of the vitriol that passed for family communication, the inevitability of the next fight. Would they all end up like his father and uncle, burned on their mysterious funeral pyre, while the whole world looked on sagely and observed that they'd brought it upon themselves? Violent lives, desperate acts—it all led to a terrible end. The cycle went on and on and on.

And was Alessandro really any different? Carlo Corretti had never met a person he wouldn't exploit for his own purposes. He'd never been honest when he could cheat, had never used persuasion when violence worked instead, and he'd never cared in the least that his hands were covered in blood.

"Right and wrong are what I say they are," he'd told Alessandro once, after ten-year-old Alessandro had walked in on him with one of his mistresses. There hadn't been the slightest hint of conscience in his gaze as he'd sprawled there in the bed he shared with Carmela. Right there in the family home. "Are you going to tell me any different, boy?"

Alessandro had hated him. God, how he'd hated him.

He looked up as if he could see Elena through the floors that separated them. She deserved better than this, and he knew it. She wasn't the Battaglia girl, auctioned off by her father to the highest bidder and fully aware of what joining the Corretti family meant—even if, as it turned out, she'd preferred a different Corretti. Elena had already escaped Niccolo Falco and whatever grim fate he'd had in store for her.

If he was any kind of man, if he was truly not like his viciously conniving father, he would set her free immediately.

Instead, he'd manipulated her, and he'd done it deliberately. She didn't have to marry him to be safe; he had teams of lawyers who could help her and her village. Who could deal with the likes of Niccolo Falco in the course of a single morning.

His mother was right. He was following in his father's

footsteps. He couldn't pretend any differently. But in the end, even that didn't matter. He wanted her too much, too badly, to do what he knew was right.

He would do his penance instead, as small as it was in the grand scheme of things. He would keep his hands off her until he married her. He would torture himself, and pretend that made this all right. That it made him something other than what he was: his father's son.

Alessandro simply didn't have it in him to let her go.

Four days later, by a special license she hadn't asked how he'd managed to obtain, Elena married Alessandro Corretti in a small civil ceremony.

It was 10:35 in the morning, in a small village outside of Palermo that Elena had never heard of before. But then, she didn't know the name of the man who married them, either, though he had introduced himself as the local mayor. Nor did she know either of the two witnesses who stood with them, both happy to take handfuls of Alessandro's euros for so little of their time.

It took all of twenty minutes.

In the private antechamber even more of Alessandro's money had secured for them, Elena stared at herself in the room's small mirror and ran her fingers down the front of the dress she wore. It was a rich, deep cream. It had delicate sleeves and fell from a pretty scooped neck into a flattering A-line that ended at her knees. Her hair was twisted back into a sophisticated chignon, and she wore a single strand of stunning pearls around her throat to match the diamond-and-pearl clusters at her ears. She looked elegant and chic. Polished. Smart.

She looked nothing at all like herself.

And why should you? a caustic voice inside her demanded. Elena Calderon was no more. She was Alessandro's wife now. *Signora Elena Corretti.*

She swallowed against the tide of emotion she didn't dare examine here, and chanced a look in Alessandro's direction. He was her husband. *Her husband.*

But he didn't love her.

Better to deal with the repercussions of that sooner rather than later, she thought, bracing herself. Better to ensure she didn't fall prey to her own imagination, her own precarious hopes. And what better place to make everything between them perfectly clear than the lounge of a town hall in a sleepy village, fitted with two ugly chairs and a desperate-looking sofa arranged around a cracked wood floor?

Congratulations on your hasty and secretive wedding, Signora Corretti, she mocked herself. *No expense or luxury was spared for your happy day!*

Alessandro stood near the closed door, on his mobile. The phone had beeped some thirty seconds after they'd signed the register. He'd announced he needed to take the call, and had waved her back into the antechamber she'd used before the ceremony.

She was almost positive she'd seen pity on the mayor's face before Alessandro had closed the door behind them.

"When do you think we should divorce?" she asked briskly when he ended his call, looking out through the small windows at the Sicilian countryside. Proud mountains with vineyards etched into the lower slopes. Red-roofed houses clinging to green hillsides. Olive groves and ancient ruins. All of it piercingly, hauntingly lovely. There was no reason at all it should have made her chest ache. "Did you have a particular time frame in mind?"

When he didn't respond, Elena turned away from the window—

And found him staring at her in amazement.

"We have been married for ten minutes, Elena," he said in a voice that made her skin pull tight. "Possibly fifteen. This conversation seems a trifle premature."

"This was the only reasonable choice I had, as you pointed out, and a convenient way to fix the Niccolo problem." She was suddenly too aware of the rings he'd slid onto her finger—a trio of flawless diamonds set in platinum on the drive over, and a diamond-studded platinum band during the ceremony, such as it was. It occurred to her that she was, in fact, deeply furious with him. She'd wanted this to mean something. She'd wanted it to matter. She was an idiot. "Nothing more than that. What does it matter if we discuss it now?"

He went incandescent. She actually saw him catch fire. His dark eyes were ferocious, his mouth flattened, and she was certain she could hear his skin sizzle with the burn of his temper from across the tiny room.

And it didn't scare her. She welcomed it. It was a happy alternative to the icy cold CEO who'd taken Alessandro's place since they'd returned to Sicily. Since the paparazzi had found them and plastered their faces across every gossip magazine and website in Europe. Since he'd shocked her with his proposal. He'd been distant. Controlled. He hadn't laid a finger on her, and there'd been nothing but winter in his dark green eyes.

She preferred this Alessandro. She knew this Alessandro.

No matter how tight and close it felt suddenly, in such a small room, with him blocking the only exit.

"I suggest you drop this subject," he advised her, hoarse with the force of his temper. There was that glitter of high passion, furious desire, in his too-dark eyes, and she exulted in it. She needed it.

"Oh," she said brightly, unable to help herself. "Were you thinking an annulment would work better?"

He laughed. It was a hard, male sound, primitive and stirring. It coursed through her, made her shiver with the heat of it. Made her ache. And the look he turned on her then melted her bones.

"I did warn you," he said.

He reached behind him and locked the door, and Elena felt it like a bullet. Hard and true, straight into her core. He crossed the room in a single stride, hauled her to him and then pulled her down with him as he sat on the sad, old sofa. Then he simply lifted her over his lap.

He hiked her dress up over her hips, ripped her panties out of his way with a casual ferocity that made her deliciously weak, then stroked two long fingers into the melting furnace of her core. Elena gasped his name. He laughed again at the evidence of how much she wanted him, all of her molten desire in his hand. She braced her hands on the smooth lapels of his wedding suit, another stunning work of art in black, and not half as beautiful as that mad hunger that changed his face, made him that much starker. Fiercer.

Hers.

Alessandro didn't look away from her as he reached between them and freed himself. He didn't look away as he ripped open a foil packet with his teeth and rolled protection on with one hand. And he didn't look away as he thrust hard into her, pulling her knees astride him, gripping her bottom in his hard hands to move her as he liked.

"An annulment is out of the question," he told her, his voice like fire, roaring through her. "And in case you're confused, this is called consummation."

Elena's head fell back as she met his thrusts, rode him, met his passion with every roll of her hips. She felt taken and glorious and his.

Completely his.

He changed the angle of her hips, moving her against him in a wicked rhythm, and she felt herself start to slip toward that edge. That easily. That quickly. Still fully dressed. Still wearing her wedding shoes and the pearls he'd presented her this morning. Still madly in love with this hard, dangerous man who was deep inside of her and knew exactly how to make her blind with desire. This man who was somehow her husband.

Whatever that meant. However long it lasted. Right then, she didn't care.

"You are mine, Elena," he whispered fiercely, his voice dark and sinful, lighting her up like a new blaze. "You are my wife."

It was that word that hurled her over, sent her flying apart in his arms, forced to muffle her cries with her own hand as he muttered something hot and dark and then followed right behind her.

When she came back to herself, he was watching her face, and she wondered in a surge of panic what he might have seen there. What she might have revealed.

"Don't talk to me about divorce," he said in a low voice, his dark green eyes hot. "Not today."

He shifted forward, setting her on her feet before him. She felt unsteady. Utterly wrecked, yet a glance in the mirror showed he hadn't disturbed a single hair on her perfectly coiffed head. She smoothed her dress back down into place, her hands trembling slightly. Alessandro tucked himself back into his trousers and then reached down to scoop up the lace panties he'd torn off her.

Because he'd been too desperate, too determined to get inside her, to wait another instant. She didn't know why that should make her feel more cherished, more precious to him, than all twenty strange minutes of their wedding ceremony.

She held out her hand to take the panties back. His hard mouth curved, his dark eyes a sensual challenge and something far more intense, and then he tucked them in his pocket.

"A memento of our wedding day," he said, mocking her, she was sure. "I'll treasure it."

She smiled back at him, cool and sharp.

"An annulment it is, then," she said. "This has been such a useful, rational discussion, Alessandro. Thank you."

He laughed again then, almost beneath his breath, and then he was on his feet and striding for the door, as if he didn't trust himself to stay locked in this room with her a moment longer. She allowed herself a small, satisfied smile.

"We can argue about this in the car," he said over his shoulder. "I have a one o'clock meeting I can't miss."

Because, of course, the CEO of Corretti Media didn't stop doing business on his wedding day, not when the wedding meant so little to him. Her smile vanished. It was a brutal reminder of reality. Of her place. It didn't matter how hot they burned. It didn't matter how desperate he'd been. Elena clenched her hands into fists and felt the bite of the unfamiliar bands around her finger like one more slap.

And then followed him, anyway.

His mobile beeped again as they walked. He answered it, slowing down as he talked. Elena heard the words *docklands, cousin* and *Battaglia*. Alessandro pushed open the glass doors at the entrance of the village hall, and nodded her through, almost as if he had a chivalrous bone in that powerful body of his.

"Wait for me in the car," he said, and then turned back toward the interior of the hall. Dismissing her.

The door swished shut behind her as she stepped

through it, and Elena pulled in a long, deep breath. The morning was still as bright and cheerful as it had been when she'd walked inside. A lovely July day in the rolling hills of Sicily. The perfect day for a wedding.

She had to figure out how to handle this, to enjoy it while it lasted, or she'd never survive it. And she had to do it fast.

Elena kept her eyes on the stairs below her as she climbed down the hall's steps, her legs still so shaky and the heels she wore no help at all, so she had to hold tight to the bannister as she went. Cracking her head open on the pavement would hardly improve matters.

She made it to the bottom step in one piece, and started to walk around the man who stood there, his back to the hall. Alessandro's sleek black sports car was parked near the fountain in the center of the pretty village square, the convertible top pulled back, reminding her of how silly she'd been on the drive over—glancing at the way the ring sparkled on her hand, allowing herself to yearn for impossibilities.

"Excuse me," she murmured absently as she navigated her way around the man, glancing at him to smile politely—

But it was Niccolo.

All of the blood drained out of her head. Her stomach contracted in a sickening lurch, and she was sure her heart dropped out of her body and lay at her feet on the pavement.

"Niccolo…" she whispered in disbelief.

Niccolo, like all of the nightmares that had kept her awake these past months. Niccolo, his arms folded over his chest and his black eyes burning mean and cold as he soaked in her reaction.

Niccolo, who she'd thought she loved until Alessandro

had walked into her life and showed her how pale that love was, how small. Niccolo, who she'd trusted. Who she'd laughed with, thinking they were laughing together. Who she'd dreamed with, thinking they were planning a shared future. Niccolo, who had hunted her across all these months and the span of Italy, and was looking at her now as if that slap in his villa was only the very beginning of what he'd like to do to her.

She couldn't believe this was happening. Today. Here. Now.

"Elena," he said, his voice almost friendly, but she could see that nasty gleam in his eyes. She could see exactly who he was. "At last."

CHAPTER TEN

ELENA NEEDED TO say something, *do* something.

Scream for help, at the very least. Kick off her shoes and run. She needed to get as far away from Niccolo as possible, to distance herself from that vicious retribution she saw shining in his black eyes and all across his boyishly handsome face.

But she couldn't seem to move a single muscle.

His lip curled. "Did you really think you could outrun me forever?"

She threw a panicked glance back up the stairs. Alessandro was still there, on the far side of the glass door, but he had his back turned to the square. To what was happening. To her.

Elena didn't know why she'd believed he could save her from this, even for an instant. Hadn't she always known she would have to handle it herself?

Niccolo looked up at Alessandro, then back at her, and his expression grew uglier.

"You've never been anything but a useless little whore, Elena," he said, his black eyes bright with malevolence. "I took you out of that fishing boat you grew up in. I made something out of you. And this is how you repay me?"

Elena straightened. Pulled in a breath. He was shorter than she remembered. Thicker and more florid. The observation gave her a burst of strength, because it meant things had changed—*she* had changed.

"You didn't do any of that for my benefit," she said, finding steel inside her, somewhere. "You did it because you wanted the land. And then you hit me."

"You owed me that land," he snarled at her. "I dressed you up, took the stink of fish out of your skin. And then you let a Corretti steal it."

"He didn't steal anything," she told him, keeping her gaze steady on his. "And he hasn't hit me, either."

"Just how long were you sleeping with him?" Niccolo demanded. "I know you lied to me. There's no way that night was the first time you met him. How long were you stringing me along?"

"You *hit* me, Niccolo," she said fiercely. "You threatened me. You lied to my family. You—"

"I let you off easy," he interrupted her, and the names he called her then, one after the next, were vile. They made her feel sick—and sicker still that she had ever loved this man, that she'd touched him, that she'd failed to see what he really was. "What I want to know is how Corretti feels every time he takes a piece of my leavings."

His hand flashed out and he grabbed her arm in a painful grip, but she didn't make a sound. She didn't even flinch. She refused to give him the satisfaction of thinking he'd hurt her again.

"Does he know, Elena?" he snarled. "Does he know I've already been there?" He smirked, smug and mean. "He's not the kind of man who likes to share."

Something in her changed then. She felt it shift. Elena didn't care that his fingers around her arm hurt. She didn't care that the look on his face would have frightened her once.

She didn't have to be afraid of him any longer. She

didn't have to run. Alessandro had given her that much. As she looked up at Niccolo now, Elena finally accepted that even if Niccolo had been who he'd pretended to be, it still would have been over between them.

It had been over the moment she'd met Alessandro.

Even if she'd never seen him again after that night in Rome, she would have known the truth: that she'd loved a stranger for the duration of a dance far more than she'd loved her fiancé. It would have ended her engagement one way or another. Maybe, she thought then, she'd actually been lucky that dance had forced Niccolo to reveal himself. It would have been much, much harder to leave the man she'd thought he was.

"But then," Niccolo was saying, "he doesn't care about you, does he? He wants the land. Do you think he would trouble himself to marry you otherwise?"

He shook her, and that hurt, too, but she didn't try to pull away. She didn't defend Alessandro's motives or worry that she didn't know what they were. She didn't cry or protest. She stared at him, memorizing this, so she would never forget what it felt like the moment she'd not only stopped being afraid of Niccolo Falco, but stopped feeling guilty about how this had all happened in the first place.

Inevitable, something whispered inside of her. *This was all inevitable.*

"I never would have married you," she said then, her voice smooth and strong. "Alessandro only expedited things. You would have shown your true face sooner or later. And I would have left you the moment I saw it."

"Look at where you are," Niccolo ground out, his fingers digging into her arm. "This tiny town, all alone. Have you really convinced yourself that a man like Alessandro Corretti, who invited half of Europe to his last wedding, cares about a nobody like you?" He laughed. "Wake up,

Elena. The only difference between Alessandro Corretti and me is that he has enough money to be a better liar."

Elena would have to think about that, she knew. She would have to investigate the damage he'd caused with that hard, low blow. But not now. Not here.

"You don't need to concern yourself with that land," she said, ignoring the rest of it. She let him see how little she feared him, let him see she wasn't shaking or cowering. "It will never be yours. You lost it the moment you thought you could hit me."

His face flushed even redder, even angrier than before. He yanked her closer to him, shoving his face into hers, trying to intimidate her with his size and strength. He was a petty man, a vicious one. But she still wasn't afraid.

"I'm not scared of you anymore, Niccolo," she said very distinctly, tilting her head back to look him full in the face. Not hiding. Not running. Not afraid. "And that means you need to let go of my arm. Now."

Whatever he saw in her face then made him drop her arm as if she'd turned into a demon right there in front of him. And Elena smiled, a real and genuine smile, because she was free of him.

After all this time, she was finally free of him.

"Step away from my wife, Falco."

Alessandro's icily furious voice cracked like a whip, startling Elena. Better, it made Niccolo move back. Alessandro was beside her then, his hand stroking down her back, as if he was reassuring himself that she still stood in one piece.

Or, the cynical part of her whispered, *marking his territory.*

"Give us a minute."

It took Elena a moment to realize that Alessandro was

speaking to her as he stared at Niccolo, murder in his dark green gaze. She frowned up at him.

But the Alessandro she knew was gone. There was nothing but darkness and vengeance on his fierce face. The promise of violence, of blood. Like a black hole where the man she loved should have been. It made every hair on the back of her neck prickle in warning. It made her pulse pick up speed.

It made her want to cry, as if they'd lost something.

"Alessandro, please," she said softly. "He's not worth it."

Niccolo sneered. Alessandro only seemed to grow bigger, taller. Darker. More terrifying. And she'd never seen his face so cold, those dark green eyes so remote.

"Alessandro," she said again.

But he still didn't look at her.

"Get in the car," he ordered her in a voice she'd never heard before. As if the man she knew was gone and in his place was this frigid and furious stranger, capable of anything. As if Niccolo was right, and she didn't know him at all. As if she never had. "Do it now."

And she didn't know how to reach him, or if she could. She didn't understand what was happening here, only that she shouldn't let him do the things she saw promised on his hard face, in those deadly eyes....

But he didn't love her. She was a temporary wife, at best.

And for all she knew, he'd married her for the land and this was simply another truth she'd been too blind to see. His true face, after all.

It ripped her up inside, but she obeyed him.

Alessandro wanted to kill Niccolo Falco. Very, very slowly.

"My congratulations," the little pissant sneered, puffing out his chest and stepping suicidally close. "You keep her on a tight leash."

His father would have simply kicked in one of Niccolo's kneecaps, the better to drag him off and beat the life out of him in a more private place. Alessandro had seen Carlo do exactly that when he was fourteen.

"Men deal with problems like men, boy," Carlo had told him, clearly disappointed that Alessandro hadn't reacted better. "Take that scared look off your face. You're a Corretti. Act like one."

And Alessandro had never felt more like a Corretti, with all of the blood and graft and misery that implied, than he did right now.

Retribution. Revenge. Finally, he understood both.

"Be very careful," Alessandro said through his teeth, trying to push back the red haze that obscured his vision. "You're talking about my wife."

Niccolo's neck was flushed. His black eyes were slits of rage, and his thick hands were in fists. Alessandro knew he'd used one of those meaty hands on Elena, once before and once today, and had to battle back the urge to break the both of them.

He had no doubt at all that he could. He hadn't fought in over forty days now—but he wasn't drunk this time.

"I had her first," Niccolo threw at him, a sly look in his eyes. "In every possible—"

"I won't warn you again."

It would be so easy. To simply end this man, as he richly deserved. He was nothing but a parasite, a lowlife. Alessandro didn't even have to get his hands dirty, the way his father had so enjoyed. He knew which former associates of his father's he could call to "handle" this. It was part and parcel of his blackened family legacy. It would take a single phone call.

This was who he was. Just as his mother had told him.

Just as Elena had accused him. Just as he had always feared.

But this would be justice, that seductive darkness whispered. *Simple. Earned.*

Alessandro had to force air into his lungs. All the choices his father and uncle and grandfather had made, all the blood that stained their hands as they'd built this family up from nothing and punished whoever dared stand in their way—he'd always looked down on them for it.

He'd never understood how easy it might be to step across that line. He'd never understood the temptation. Or that it could seem not only right to exterminate a cockroach like Niccolo Falco, but inarguably just.

Necessary.

That darkness in him didn't even seem particularly dark to him today as he stared at the bastard who'd terrorized Elena. It seemed like a choice. The right choice.

But.

But Elena had cried in his arms, and then she'd trusted him when he didn't deserve it at all. When he'd given her no reason to trust him. She'd married him. He couldn't understand why she'd done it. He wasn't sure he ever would.

But it burned in him. It lived in him, bright like hope.

"Be the man who does the right thing," she'd said once. And her eyes were the perfect blue of all his favorite summers, and she'd looked at him as if he could never be a man like his father.

As if she had some kind of faith in him, after all.

"Why take her at all?" Niccolo demanded, stepping even closer, tempting fate. "Because she was mine?"

Alessandro smiled at him, cold and vicious. "Because I can."

Niccolo snorted. "You're nothing but a thug in fancy clothes, aren't you?"

Alessandro was done then. With Niccolo, with all of this. With who he'd nearly become. With that dark spiral he'd almost lost himself in today, that he could still feel inside of him.

But Elena was like light, and he wanted her more.

"Don't let me see you again, Falco. Don't even cross into my line of sight. You won't like what happens." He leaned closer then, pleased in a purely primitive way that he was bigger. Taller. That there was that flicker of fear in the other man's eyes. "And stay the hell away from my wife. That goes for you and your entire pathetic family. You do not want to go to war with me, I promise you."

Niccolo recoiled, the angry flush on his face and neck bleeding into something darker. Nastier.

"Don't worry," he said, ugly and flat. "Once I'm finished with a whore—"

Alessandro shut him up. With his fist.

He felt the crunch of bone that told him he'd broken Niccolo's nose, heard the other man's bellow of pain as he crumpled to the ground. Where he lay in a cowardly heap, clutching at his face.

And Alessandro wasn't his father, he would never be his father, but he was still Corretti enough to enjoy it.

"Next time," he promised, "I won't be so kind."

And then he walked away and left Niccolo Falco bleeding into the ground.

But alive.

"I'm sorry I let him touch you," Alessandro said gruffly when he swung into the car. Elena sat there so primly in the passenger seat, looking perfect. Untouchable. Her face smooth and her eyes hidden away behind dark glasses. "It won't happen again."

"He didn't hurt me," she said. Far too politely. When he

only frowned at her, searching her face for some sign, she shifted slightly in her seat. "Don't you have a meeting?"

He reminded himself that he had her torn panties in his pocket. That if he reached over and touched her, he could have her moaning out his name in moments. But he started the car instead, and pulled out onto the small country road that led away from the village and back toward Palermo.

He'd told her Niccolo wouldn't come for her, and he had. She had every right to be afraid, even angry. To blame him.

He could handle that. He could handle anything—because she'd married him, and they had nothing now but time. The rest of their lives, rolling out before them. There was nowhere to hide. Not for long.

They drove in silence, the warm summer day rushing all around them, sunshine and wind dancing in and around the car. The hills were green and pretty and off in the distance the sea beckoned. She was his wife, and he wasn't his father.

It might not be perfect, Alessandro thought. It might take some work yet. But it was good.

"Why did you hit him?" she asked as they started to make their way into the city sprawl, and the wind no longer prohibited conversation.

"I should have killed him," Alessandro replied shortly. "I wanted to kill him."

But he hadn't.

He hadn't.

"I didn't say he didn't deserve it," she replied in that cool way that he still hated, even now. "I only wondered what horrible thing he might have said to tip you over that edge."

Alessandro eyed her as he stopped at a traffic light. He considered telling her about real edges, and what lay on the other side of them, but refrained. There would be time enough to introduce her to all the poison and pain that was his birthright, to tell her what had happened back there and what he'd finally rejected once and for all.

"He called you a whore."

"Ah," she said. She sat there so elegantly. So calmly. Her hands folded in her lap, her legs neatly crossed. She smiled, and it scraped at him. "So it's only okay when you do it?"

Alessandro pulled in a breath through his teeth.

"Damn it, Elena," he began, but she turned to face the front again, and nodded toward the road with every appearance of serenity.

"The light's changed."

He swore in Sicilian as well as Italian, and then he drove with more fury than skill through the city, screeching to a halt at the valet in front of the Corretti Media tower.

Elena let herself out of the car before he had the chance to come around and get her, starting toward the building's entrance as if she didn't care one way or the other if he followed her. Gritting his teeth, he did.

She said nothing as they walked through the marble lobby. She only slid her dark glasses onto the top of her head and let him guide her into the elevator when it arrived.

"Is there anything else you plan to throw at me today?" he asked, tamping down on his temper as the doors slid shut. "Do we need to have another discussion like the one we had about divorce?"

Elena stared straight ahead, her gaze fixed on the far wall and the flashing numbers that announced each floor, though a faint flush spread across her cheeks.

"There's nothing else," she said. He didn't recognize that voice she used, the way she held herself. But he knew she was lying. "I'm sorry. I don't know why I said that."

"Are you sure he didn't hurt you?" he asked quietly.

She looked at him then, and her blue eyes were shadowed. Dark.

"No." There was something there then. Something making her voice catch, her mouth take on that hint of vulnerability that killed him. "I told you."

"Elena," he said. "You have to know—"

But his mobile beeped. She blinked, then looked away, and when she glanced at him again her face was that smooth mask. He couldn't stand it.

"Tell me what's wrong," he urged her. "Tell me what happened."

"You should answer that," she said, much too calmly, when his phone kept beeping. "I'm sure it's important."

He pulled out the phone to look at the screen, and wasn't surprised at the number he saw flashing there.

"It's my family," he started, not knowing how to compress the history of the Corretti feuds into something coherent. Not knowing how he felt about any of it, now that he'd pulled himself back from the abyss that had stalked him all these years. "There are all these divisions, these petty little wars—"

"I read the papers, Alessandro," she said gently. "I know about your family." She nodded at his mobile. "You should take the call."

"I always take the call," he gritted out. "And it never helps. Whenever there's a possibility of ending this nonsense, we make sure to destroy it." He shook his head. "I'm beginning to believe we always will."

She looked at him for a long moment, and he had the sense she was weighing something behind those stormy eyes he couldn't read. She reached over and hit one of the elevator buttons, making his main office floor light up.

"Then you should fix it," she said. She even smiled, and it was almost real. He almost believed she meant it. "Isn't that what you do?"

"No," he said shortly, his gaze searching hers. "Obviously not."

Her eyes were much too dark, and it ate at him. Something flared between them in the small space, a different kind of fire, and he had the awful sense that he'd already lost her. That she had already disappeared.

But she was right here, he reminded himself sternly. She had married him slightly more than an hour ago. She was his.

"What's the right thing?" she asked, her voice too quiet. "Do that, even if it hurts. Your family deserves it."

"And if they don't?"

After all these bitter years. After all the pain, the blood.

He thought he saw compassion in her gaze, or maybe he only wanted that. Maybe he was simply desperate for something he recognized, something to ease the gnawing sensation inside of him.

The elevator doors slid open, and she looked away, out toward the hushed executive level of Corretti Media.

His phone beeped again. Insistent. Annoying. He heard Giovanni's voice from the office floor, the valet no doubt having informed him that Alessandro had returned.

"Your family might not deserve it, Alessandro. But you do."

"Me?" He hardly made a sound. He hardly breathed. "I fear I deserve it least of all."

The moment stretched between them, taut and shimmering with all the things he did not, could not, feel, except for her. He said her name again. His favorite incantation. His only remaining prayer.

"Go," she whispered.

And it wasn't until the elevator door had closed on her, and he was striding toward his responsibilities the way he always did, that he realized what he'd seen flash in her eyes then was a deep, dark sadness.

Elena took an early-afternoon flight out of Palermo's Falcone Borcellino Airport, headed for Naples and the car she'd hired for the drive back to her village. She settled into the economy-class seat she'd bought with the money she'd earned waitressing and on Alessandro's yacht, not the money he—or, more likely, his staff—had left for her in the penthouse in a folder with her name on the front and a selection of credit cards and cash within.

And when the plane took off and soared into the air above Sicily, she didn't let herself look back.

"Because I can," he'd said to Niccolo. That was why he'd danced with her. That was why he'd done all of this. Married her. Just as she'd suspected, it was all a game. Because he could.

She hadn't thought she'd hear him admit it.

And as she'd sat in his car in the sun-drenched village square, twisting all of those diamonds around and around on her finger, Niccolo's harsh words circling in her head, she'd had to face the facts she'd been avoiding for far too long.

She'd been so sure that she, Elena Calderon, *deserved* what Niccolo had represented. That she *should* be the one chosen from all the girls in the village to swan off into a posh life, dripping in gowns and villas.

Alessandro had been right to accuse her of that, but wrong about why—and around him it was even worse. He was the most powerful man she'd ever met. His ruthlessness was equal parts intimidating and exciting. He was beautiful and lethal, and he'd wanted her as desperately as she'd wanted him.

Some part of her obviously believed that she deserved

no less than the CEO of one of the most successful media corporations in Europe. That she deserved rings made of diamonds, private islands and a three-story penthouse perched over Palermo like an opulent aerie.

How remarkably conceited she was.

She remembered then, as the plane winged across the blue sea, one of the last nights they'd spent on the island. They'd sat together on the beach, watching the sunset. He'd been behind her, letting her sprawl between his legs and against his chest.

He'd played with her hair and she'd watched the sun sink toward the horizon. She'd felt so filled with hope. So unreasonably optimistic.

Until she'd recalled the last time she'd felt that way.

It had been the night of that fateful charity ball. She'd finished dressing in the new, beautiful gown Niccolo had chosen for her, and she'd been unable to stop staring at herself in the mirror of their hotel suite. She'd looked so glamorous, so sophisticated. And she'd felt the same sense of well-being, of happiness, roll through her.

This is exactly how my life should be, she'd thought then.

On the beach with Alessandro, she'd shivered.

"What's the matter?" he'd asked, tugging gently on her hair so she'd look back at him. The reds and golds of the setting sun cast him in bronze, once again like a very old god, perfect and deadly.

"Nothing," she'd lied, and she'd wanted it to be nothing. Just an odd coincidence. No reason at all for that sudden hollow pit in her stomach.

He'd smiled, and kissed her, then he'd wrapped his arms around her like a man in love and had tucked her under his chin in that way she adored, and she'd known without a shadow of a doubt that it was no coincidence. That it had been a sign, and she'd do well to heed it.

That when the forty days were up she had to leave him. *She had to.*

And she'd gone ahead and married him, anyway.

But then, she thought now, shifting in her narrow seat, every decision she'd made for more than half a year she'd made out of fear.

Fear of what Niccolo would do to her. Fear of her parents' disappointment. Fear of losing Alessandro—a man who had insulted her upon their first meeting, thought the very worst of her even as he slept with her, and had even married her in undue, secretive haste in a sleepy little village where no one knew him.

Niccolo was a disgusting creep, but he'd had a point.

And the truth was, though she never would have phrased it the way he had, she would always smell of fish and hard, thankless work like the people she came from. No matter what airs she tried to put on, what gowns or jewels she wore, she was a village girl. She had no place with a man like Alessandro.

More than that, he was a Corretti.

Maybe Alessandro really was the man he claimed he was, a man who strove to do what was right no matter what his family name. She thought of that painful conversation in the elevator and she ached—because she wanted so badly to believe him. To believe that the darkness she'd seen in him today was an aberration, not the true face he'd kept from her the way Niccolo had.

Maybe.

But she had to accept that it was just as likely that he was exactly who Niccolo had told her he was. Exactly who she'd believed he was.

It was time to go home. It was time to stop playing at games she hardly understood. It was past time.

Elena needed to face up to what she'd done. She needed

to beg for her parents' forgiveness—not for calling off one wedding, not for marrying yet another man who might very well ruin everything, but for not trusting them enough. For not staying and fighting the lies Niccolo had told. For not believing that they could love her enough to overcome their disappointment in her. For running away instead.

It had solved nothing. It had been a selfish, scared act. It had hurt the people who loved her. And it had broken her heart.

The land was out of her hands, she thought now, her eyes easing closed as she accepted that bitter reality. As she acknowledged her own failure. In the end, it was only land. Dirt and stones and trees. It wasn't worth all of this suffering.

Elena had to believe that.

She closed the window shade beside her so she wouldn't give in to the temptation to look back, shut her eyes tight and prayed she'd make it home in time.

CHAPTER ELEVEN

ALESSANDRO SAT ALONE in his office on the executive floor of the Corretti Media tower. His mobile beeped insistently at him, but he ignored it. Just as he ignored the new proposal Giovanni had drafted for him, comprising Alessandro's bid for the cursed docklands regeneration project. All he needed to do was sign it.

And then, of course, persuade Alessia Battaglia's grasping, two-faced father to honor the commitment he'd made back when Alessandro and Alessia had agreed to marry.

But instead he'd cleared his office.

The proposal was one more gauntlet thrown down in this same old war. It cut out his cousins completely, following right along in Carlo's footsteps, adhering to the same script his father and uncle had written in their blood decades back.

Alessandro pushed back from his desk and roamed restlessly around his great office, a suitable corporate celebration of a man of his wealth, power and position. It was a space meant to intimidate. To assert in no uncertain terms the full weight and heft of Corretti authority.

That goddamned name.

He walked to the windows, and looked out over the city of his birth. Palermo basked before him in the summer sun, corrupt and decaying, beautiful and serene. A mass of contradictions imprinted with the fingerprints of history, this place; streets marked with violence surrounding ancient green squares of breathtaking loveliness. Byzantine churches, leftover city walls, influences ranging from the Phoenicians to the Mafia. And it was inside of him. It was home. Unlike his brother, he had never wanted to live abroad. Sicily sang in his blood. Palermo was the key to who he was.

And who he was, who he had always been, was a Corretti.

But he was no longer sure what that meant.

He could have become his father at any time in all these years. He could have stepped all too easily into Carlo's shoes today. He'd finally felt what that would mean. He'd wanted it. He'd even thought Niccolo Falco deserved it.

But the woman who'd told him that he deserved what was right, whatever that was, deserved better than a violent criminal as her husband. And it made him question not only himself, but this whole notion of who the Correttis were. If it was a curse, this name—or it was merely one more choice they all kept making.

Today Alessandro had chosen not to take the easy way, the corrupt and criminal way. His father's way. He'd spent his life believing he did what was right, that he did his duty.

Now it was time to prove it.

He walked back over to his desk and shoved the proposal out of his way, picking up his mobile to make two calls he should have made years ago. To offer, if not an olive branch, a start. A fresh, clean start.

His duty to his family should be about the living, not the dead. The Corretti name should not be forever synonymous with the actions of those long buried.

Because the past didn't matter. What mattered were the choices they made now. He, his half-brother, Angelo, and his cousin Matteo shouldn't have to follow along in the footsteps of monsters, simply because those monsters were their fathers. And they certainly didn't have to become them.

Surely, he told himself, they could simply…stop this.

His cousin Matteo picked up the phone, and Alessandro braced himself for a necessary, if excruciatingly awkward, conversation.

It was only as dark as they allowed it to be, he thought. And it was long past time for the light.

Elena let herself out of her parents' house high up on the rocky hillside, and pulled the door closed behind her quietly, so as not to disturb her father's rest. It was a gray, foggy morning, the air thick and cool against her skin. She pulled her old jacket tighter around her, and set off down the slanting street.

She felt turned inside out. Rubbed entirely raw. Her parents had done nothing but love her since her return yesterday afternoon. Her mother had wept. Her father had smiled as if she was a blessing from on high. Elena was humbled. Grateful.

And she'd still been unable to sleep, her mind and her body torturing her with memories of Alessandro. Images of Alessandro. All of that heat and light, fire and need.

She'd learned nothing.

The sloping streets and ancient stone stairs that led the way down the hillside were second nature to her. Each house, each alley, each clothesline hanging naked in today's weather, was like its own separate greeting. This was home. It had always been home. She was made to smell of the sea, the salt and the sun and the bounty they provided. There was no shame in that.

Yet today she felt out of place in a way she never had before.

It will come, she assured herself as she came to the bottom of the steep hill that led into the main square. *You've been away for a long time.*

Everything seemed different in the thick mist. Sounds were muffled, and strange echoes seemed to nip at her heels. She narrowly avoided one of the village's biggest gossips, darting around the far side of the great statue that sat in the center of the square, and was so busy looking back over her shoulder to be sure she'd escaped that she ran right into someone.

Elena opened her mouth to apologize, but she knew that rock-hard chest. She knew the strong hands that wrapped around her upper arms and righted her.

It seemed to take a thousand years to lift her gaze to his, to confirm what she already knew.

What her body was already celebrating, with an insistent ache in her heart and core alike.

"What are you doing here?" she gasped out.

Alessandro's wicked brows rose in arrogant amazement. "You left me."

"I had to come home," she blurted out in a rush, the strangest urge to apologize to him, to offer him comfort, working its way through her. Proving, she thought, her terrible weakness. "And what does it matter to you?"

"You left me," he said again, each word distinct and furious.

Elena ignored the things that clamored in her then, all of that fear and despair that she'd lost him, all of her desperate, foolish love for a man she couldn't have. Not really. Not the way she wanted him.

"Is this about the land?" she asked baldly. "Because you

didn't have to come all the way here for that. You don't have to pretend anymore."

His eyes blazed, so lethally hot she took a step back, and then cursed herself for it. Alessandro was a lot of things, but he wasn't Niccolo. She knew he would never hurt her—not like that.

"It turns out," Alessandro bit out, betrayal and accusation in those dark green eyes, "that I am sick and tired of being discarded on my wedding day."

Elena paled, then reddened.

"Not here," she managed to get out.

She ducked into one of the ancient passageways that wound around behind a few of the shops and deposited them on a lonely stretch of the rocky cliffs overlooking the small harbor. And then she faced him.

He stood there, dark and furious, dressed in one of those impossibly sleek suits that made him look terrifying and delicious all at once, a symphony of powerful, wealthy male beauty. It reminded her that she was only a village girl in old clothes and messy hair, no doubt smelling again of fish.

"What exactly are you doing, Elena?" he asked, his voice clipped.

"This is where I belong," she said defiantly. "This is who I am."

He only watched her, his dark green eyes narrow and fierce.

"I brought you something," he said after a moment. He reached into an inside pocket of his suit jacket and she was sure, for a dizzy moment, that he was going to pull out those torn panties and then what would she do? But instead, he handed her a thick envelope.

Elena took it, her fingers acting of their own accord, a

miserable, sinking sensation washing through her, from her throat to her heart to her belly.

"Is this—?" Her throat was so dry she could hear the words scrape as she formed them. "Are these divorce papers?"

This was what she wanted, she tried to tell herself. This was a good thing. But she wanted only to curl up somewhere and cry.

His hard mouth curved into something far too angry to be a smile.

"It's a legal document," he said, his eyes never leaving hers. "It relinquishes any claim I might have had to your family's land, and hands it back to you." Elena made a small noise, her fingers clutching almost convulsively at the envelope. "And I suggest you take note of the date. It was signed three days ago."

Meaning, it took her a confused moment to understand, that he had signed the land over to her before their wedding.

"I don't…" she whispered.

"In case there is any lingering confusion," he said in that deadly way of his, "I never wanted the goddamn land. I wanted you."

Which meant he really was the man she'd wanted him to be—but Elena couldn't process that. There was nothing but a roar of thunder inside her, loud and overwhelming.

He didn't love her, she reminded herself then, cutting through all the noise. No matter what kind of man he was.

The envelope shook in her hand. "I don't know what to say."

"What a surprise." His voice was cool, but his eyes burned hot, and she burned with them. "And here I thought your silent defection was so eloquent."

He reached out for her other hand, taking it in his, and Elena watched in stunned silence—as if it was not her hand at all, as if it was connected to someone else—as he reached into a different pocket and slid the rings she'd left in the penthouse back onto her finger.

"I don't want those," she croaked out. His hand closed around hers then, and she felt that electric charge sizzle all the way up her arm.

"They're yours," he bit out, his dark eyes flashing. "Just like the clothes you left behind. If you don't want them, fine. Sell them. Burn them in your back garden. But I won't take them back."

She yanked her hand away, as if her palm was on fire. It felt like it was. It felt like she was.

But Alessandro was a dream and it was time to wake up. She had to stop prostrating herself to impossibilities. She had to stop dreaming about what she thought she ought to have, and concentrate instead on what she did have. And that wasn't him.

"I appreciate this more than I can say," she said in a low voice, stepping back from him and tucking the envelope in the pocket of her jacket.

"All I asked was that you have a little faith," he gritted out. "Was that really so hard, Elena? Did it warrant you running away from me mere hours after our wedding?"

"We have sex," she said evenly, because it was time to accept reality. "That's all it is, Alessandro. That's all it ever was."

"You're still such a liar," he said in a kind of wonder.

"It's not real," she continued, determined to make him see reason. "It's chemical. It fades."

"We do not *just* have sex," he said, moving toward her then. "What we have, Elena, is extraordinary. It was there from the moment we met."

He reached over and slid his palm along her jaw, her cheek, anchoring his fingers in her hair. That same fire roared in her, that easily. That same old connection that had caused all this trouble. And he knew it. His mouth curved.

"You can't—" she began, but he only pressed a finger over her lips and she subsided, her heart pounding.

"And if you want something real," he said in a low, stirring voice that did nothing to conceal his temper and seemed to echo in her bones, her veins, her core, making something like shame twist in her, low and deep, "then you're going to have to treat me like I'm real, too. Not something you have to bend and contort to get around. Just a man, Elena. Nothing more or less than that."

That thudded into her, hard. She wrenched herself back, away from his touch. She fought for breath.

"You're a man, yes," she threw at him. "I know that. But your only form of communication is in bed—"

"Do not," he interrupted her furiously, "*do not* claim I can't *communicate* when your version of a discussion involves sneaking off for a plane ride and two hours' drive."

"You don't understand!" She hardly knew what she was saying. She was panicked. Cornered. "I loved you so much I was willing to do anything. I wrecked my engagement. I betrayed my family. I lost myself—anything to have you. But that's not love, Alessandro." She shook her head wildly. Desperately. "It's an addiction. *It's just sex.*"

"Thank you," he said grimly, "for using the past tense. Keep sticking your knife in, Elena. Twist it, why don't you."

But she couldn't stop. It was as if something else had taken control of her.

"We never should have met," she told him. "We were never *meant* to meet. It was a complete disaster at first sight."

"It was love at first sight," Alessandro snapped at her. "And you know it."

That was like a deep, terrible rip, so far inside her she didn't think she could survive it.

"Don't you dare say that!" she hurled at him. "Don't you dare pretend!"

"I love you!" he thundered, the words ricocheting from the stone walls of the village, the rocky cliffs, the thick fog and the water below.

Or maybe that was only in her head. Maybe that was her heart.

Alessandro found her gaze, held it. Frustration and determination gleamed there in all of that dark green, along with something else.

Sincerity, she thought, from some stunned distance. *He meant it.* She heard a small noise, a kind of gasp, and only dimly realized she'd made it.

"I love you, Elena," he said, his voice serious. Certain. "Since the moment I saw you, I've never been the same."

"You…" But she couldn't seem to speak.

"There were no contracts," he said then, fiercely. "No discussions about assets or settlements. No prenuptial agreement. I simply married you, because I can't be without you. I can't let you leave me." His dark eyes flashed. *"I can't."*

She tried to say his name, formed the syllables of it with her mouth, but no sound came out.

"I have a great darkness in me," he said then, intently. "I can't pretend I don't. But it's not going to win. It can't, if I have you."

She shook her head, as if she could shake this off. As if she could push him back into those neatly labeled boxes she'd set out for him. She had to do it, or she might die where she stood. She didn't question that—she simply knew it.

"We were always destined to burn ourselves out, Alessandro," she said when she could speak. "This was doomed from the start."

He closed the distance between them then, and took her shoulders in his hands. Kind and gentle. Heartbreakingly firm.

"Do you want me to convince you?" he asked roughly, a broken look in his dark eyes. "Is that what this is? Because we both know I can."

"What?" Her ears were ringing, louder by the second. "No, I—"

"Tell me what you *want*, Elena," he said, all of his ferocity and all of the desolation she'd sensed in him right there between them, suddenly. Alive in the damp air. "Do you *want* me to hunt you down, make you accept what's between us? Do you *want* me to leave you alone? You need to choose. You need to *fight*."

He dropped his hands then, stepped back, and the distance between them was unbearable. It made her shake.

"You can't put this all on me," he continued, his voice low but with the ring of a kind of finality that made everything inside of her twist tight in anguish.

"I don't know what I want," she lied, and the look in his eyes then shamed her. Destroyed her. Because he knew she was lying. He always knew.

"I loved you before I knew your name," he said then. "I love you more now, even when you lie to my face. All you have to do is own this, Elena."

She shuddered. She couldn't do it. She couldn't—

"I do," she said desperately. "I love you."

"I know you do," he replied, a slight curve to that hard mouth, but it wasn't enough. "But that's not the issue, is it? It never has been."

And something in her finally broke then. Pride, fear. Selfishness and vanity. All the things she'd been accused of, all the accusations she'd levied at herself. It all simply cracked into pieces and washed over her.

"I left because I couldn't bear to be so stupid," she told him in a rush. "To make such a terrible mistake again." Her eyes filled with tears, spilled over, wetting her cheeks. "But I married you because I wanted to marry you. I wanted you."

She wiped at her eyes, then focused on him, and he took up the whole world. Commanding and strong. But waiting to hear what she'd say next. What she'd decide. As if she was the one with the power, after all.

"I still do, Alessandro," she whispered. "I want you more than I've ever wanted anything else. I can't fight that. I tried."

"You don't have to fight that," he said, his dark green eyes so fierce on hers she trembled. "You don't have to fight me. Just fight *for* this, Elena. Don't run away. Don't hide."

She made a wordless sort of sound, far past the ability to speak, and he pulled her close and let her cry.

"I'm not your enemy," he murmured into her hair.

"I know," she whispered into his strong, warm chest. "I know you're not."

She shuddered against him, and then he kissed her. Sweet, sure. Hot. Like a promise. Like hope. And when he drew back she saw the future she'd been too afraid to imagine, right there in his dark eyes, that curve of his perfect mouth.

"Come back to Sicily with me," he said. "And stay this time. Stay for good."

Elena nodded, too overwhelmed to speak. And this wasn't surrender, she realized. She wasn't losing a thing. She was gaining Alessandro—she was gaining *them*.

She was trading in something broken, something ruined and outgrown, for a shared set of wings and the whole bright sky to call their own.

"I want you to meet my parents," she whispered. "My father. He's not well, but...I think he'll like you."

"That is exceedingly unlikely," he said quietly. "I'm a Corretti."

And it was Elena's turn to kiss him then, to press her mouth against his and set him free with all of that fire that was always, only theirs. To love him with nothing held back, nothing hidden. To bask in that terrible, impossible, extraordinary love that had slammed into them with no warning, changing them both. Changing everything.

"He'll love you," she told him. She looped her arms around his neck and adored the way he smiled down at her. "Because I love you. That's how it works."

He was shadow and light. Ruthless and kind. Dark green eyes and that wild, hot heat when he looked at her.

And all of him hers, as he had been from the start. From that single glance across a crowded room.

"I will always be a Corretti," Alessandro said. It was a warning. Or, she thought, a promise.

Elena smiled. "So will I."

* * * * *

Read on for an exclusive interview with Caitlin Crews!

BEHIND THE SCENES OF
SICILY'S CORRETTI DYNASTY

It's such a huge world to create—an entire Sicilian dynasty. Did you discuss parts of it with the other writers?

Oh, yes! The other writers were such a huge part of the experience for me—thank goodness, as they're all so talented! We talked about a lot of different story points, and even shared scenes when we used one another's characters. I couldn't have written it without them!

How does being part of a continuity differ from when you are writing your own stories?

It's a completely different kind of challenge. When you're writing your own books all the choices you make are organic; they all flow together as you write. In a continuity you have to work inside out, in some respects. You have to back into the characters in order to flesh them out, for example. You have to think a lot about *why* they do the things you're told they do. I'd say it's the writing equivalent of coloring in an already drawn character rather than drawing it yourself from scratch. Either way, you have to make them yours, but the process is a bit different.

What was the biggest challenge? And what did you most enjoy about it?

Learning who my characters really were was the biggest challenge—and then, when I did, I just loved them.

As you wrote your hero and heroine was there anything about them that surprised you?

Many things! I never quite knew what either of them would

say, or how dark things would get for them before they found their way back to the light.

What was your favorite part of creating the world of Sicily's most famous dynasty?

I loved Alessandro and Elena, but I also had a lot of fun researching Sicily. What a fantastic place!

If you could have given your heroine one piece of advice before the opening pages of the book, what would it be?

I would have told her to trust her heart. But we never do, do we?

What was your hero's biggest secret?

That would be telling!

What does your hero love most about your heroine?

She's seen the dark side of him and she loves him, anyway—she's not afraid of him.

What does your heroine love most about your hero?

That she can trust him to be who he says he is, and not to betray her.

Which of the Correttis would you most like to meet and why?

They're a bit intense, aren't they? I think I'd like to watch them all from afar, as they're so fascinating and gorgeous. Maybe if they were all gathered at a restaurant? Particularly one in Sicily, where I could glut myself on the wonderful food and watch a few Corretti dramas play out over the course of the meal....

ROMANCE

Million Dollar Christmas Proposal	Lucy Monroe
A Dangerous Solace	Lucy Ellis
The Consequences of That Night	Jennie Lucas
Secrets of a Powerful Man	Chantelle Shaw
Never Gamble with a Caffarelli	Melanie Milburne
Visconti's Forgotten Heir	Elizabeth Power
A Touch of Temptation	Tara Pammi
A Scandal in the Headlines	Caitlin Crews
What the Bride Didn't Know	Kelly Hunter
Mistletoe Not Required	Anne Oliver
Proposal at the Lazy S Ranch	Patricia Thayer
A Little Bit of Holiday Magic	Melissa McClone
A Cadence Creek Christmas	Donna Alward
Marry Me under the Mistletoe	Rebecca Winters
His Until Midnight	Nikki Logan
The One She Was Warned About	Shoma Narayanan
Her Firefighter Under the Mistletoe	Scarlet Wilson
Christmas Eve Delivery	Connie Cox

MEDICAL

Gold Coast Angels: Bundle of Trouble	Fiona Lowe
Gold Coast Angels: How to Resist Temptation	Amy Andrews
Snowbound with Dr Delectable	Susan Carlisle
Her Real Family Christmas	Kate Hardy

Mills & Boon® Large Print

November 2013

ROMANCE

HISTORICAL

MEDICAL

Mills & Boon® Hardback

December 2013

ROMANCE

Defiant in the Desert	Sharon Kendrick
Not Just the Boss's Plaything	Caitlin Crews
Rumours on the Red Carpet	Carole Mortimer
The Change in Di Navarra's Plan	Lynn Raye Harris
The Prince She Never Knew	Kate Hewitt
His Ultimate Prize	Maya Blake
More than a Convenient Marriage?	Dani Collins
A Hunger for the Forbidden	Maisey Yates
The Reunion Lie	Lucy King
The Most Expensive Night of Her Life	Amy Andrews
Second Chance with Her Soldier	Barbara Hannay
Snowed in with the Billionaire	Caroline Anderson
Christmas at the Castle	Marion Lennox
Snowflakes and Silver Linings	Cara Colter
Beware of the Boss	Leah Ashton
Too Much of a Good Thing?	Joss Wood
After the Christmas Party...	Janice Lynn
Date with a Surgeon Prince	Meredith Webber

MEDICAL

From Venice with Love	Alison Roberts
Christmas with Her Ex	Fiona McArthur
Her Mistletoe Wish	Lucy Clark
Once Upon a Christmas Night...	Annie Claydon

Mills & Boon® Large Print
December 2013

ROMANCE

The Billionaire's Trophy	Lynne Graham
Prince of Secrets	Lucy Monroe
A Royal Without Rules	Caitlin Crews
A Deal with Di Capua	Cathy Williams
Imprisoned by a Vow	Annie West
Duty at What Cost?	Michelle Conder
The Rings That Bind	Michelle Smart
A Marriage Made in Italy	Rebecca Winters
Miracle in Bellaroo Creek	Barbara Hannay
The Courage To Say Yes	Barbara Wallace
Last-Minute Bridesmaid	Nina Harrington

HISTORICAL

Not Just a Governess	Carole Mortimer
A Lady Dares	Bronwyn Scott
Bought for Revenge	Sarah Mallory
To Sin with a Viking	Michelle Willingham
The Black Sheep's Return	Elizabeth Beacon

MEDICAL

NYC Angels: Making the Surgeon Smile	Lynne Marshall
NYC Angels: An Explosive Reunion	Alison Roberts
The Secret in His Heart	Caroline Anderson
The ER's Newest Dad	Janice Lynn
One Night She Would Never Forget	Amy Andrews
When the Cameras Stop Rolling...	Connie Cox

1113 GEN STD LP